Adventures in
Shar

COPYRIGHT PAGE

HEIRS TO TROUBLE

Adventures in the Liaden Universe® Number 26

© Sharon Lee and Steve Miller November 2017

Pinbeam Books

www.pinbeambooks.com

Roving Gambler was first published on Splinter Universe, April 2014

Code of Honor was first published on Splinter Universe in May 2014

Both stories were collected in A Liaden Universe® Constellation Volume 3, Baen Books

August 2015

Photo by Pawel Nolbert[1] on Unsplash[2]

Cover design by Sharon Lee

ISBN: 978-0-9966346-4-9

1.   https://unsplash.com/photos/4u2U8EO9OzY?utm_source=unsplash&utm_medium=referral&utm_content=creditCopyText

2.   https://unsplash.com/?utm_source=unsplash&utm_medium=referral&utm_content=creditCopyText

A note on the existence of this echapbook. . .

Those who have been following the Liaden Universe® and/or the career of Sharon Lee and Steve Miller for a time will know that we'd gotten into the habit of producing chapbooks – 8.5x5.5 inch saddle-stitched pamphlets of 40-60 pages. The very first Lee-and-Miller chapbook was *The Naming of Kinzel*, collecting three fantasy stories featuring a well-meaning young wizard named Kinzel, which we published (it says here) in a limited run of 300, on June 20, 1987.

Later, SRM Publisher was formed, for the purpose of publishing chapbooks containing Lee-and-Miller, Miller, Lee, and, later still, other authors, work. This was in the age of paper; there were no ereaders, and computer screens were pretty rugged, still. For seventeen years, starting in 1995, SRM Publisher produced at least one chapbook a year, at Yule, containing one or two Liaden stories.

SRM was closed in 2011, and we quickly realized that we weren't going to be able to break ourselves of writing short stories, so we established Splinter Universe (http://www.splinteruniverse.com[1]), where we would occasionally publish "splinters," i.e. pieces of stories or books that never came to completion, and also any new stories we happened to write.

Ever since SRM closed its doors, there had been a call from the readers who had been with the universe and the authors through all the changes, for the return of chapbooks. By now, technology had caught up with itself, so the authors began to produce echapbooks, on the model of the first paper chapbooks – and also republished all of SRMs backlist in ebook format.

---

1.   http://www.splinteruniverse.com/

At that point, the traditional publisher of our novels, Baen Books, suggested that they collect our stories into what was at first to be one volume. We agreed, realized that one volume wasn't going to be enough – so eventually *A Liaden Universe® Constellation Volumes 1* and *2* were published from Baen.

And that, should have been that.

Except – no, we *still* couldn't break ourselves of the short story habit, and the *Constellations* had done well for Baen. As soon as we had published enough short stories to warrant a book, Baen offered a contract for *A Liaden Universe® Constellation Volume 3*, which took several stories straight off of Splinter Universe. Those stories were never collected into chapbooks.

We recently realized that this was the case, and, in the interests of completeness, we have produced two echapbooks, collecting the four stories that were missed.

This is the second of those two "catch up" echapbooks, containing two novelettes: "Roving Gambler" and "Code of Honor."

This is what we said about each of those stories, in *Constellation 3*:

Roving Gambler

At times we, as coauthors, talk about and know so much about what's going on in the universe that we forget that we haven't written it down. "Roving Gambler" came from that abundance of information – dealing with story stuff that we knew but hadn't quite managed to get into a novel or another short story yet. We have a lot of characters, and they are all involved – even if we haven't had time to write them in. So here's a story featuring Quin – we knew that Quin was isolated, we knew that the arrival of Korval on Liad was not going to be easy on the clan and on Pat Rin. Something, of course, was going to have to happen. "Roving Gambler" helps get Quin happening.

Code of Honor

This story exists because we were plotting a completely different story, and needed a character to. . .do something. . .for the main character. That secondary character came with an utterly fascinating backstory. So fascinating, in fact, that he got his own story, set in the aftermath of I Dare. And yes, we are still planning to write the story that spawned this one, so. . .watch the skies!

If this is your first time reading these stories, we do hope you enjoy them. And, for those of you re-reading, we hope you enjoy spending additional time with old friends found again.

Sharon Lee and Steve Miller

Cat Farm and Confusion Factory

November 2017

Roving Gambler

He woke instantly, more pilot than person, swinging his legs from the bed as soon as his eyes were open. The three coordinate sets in his head were good enough if there was—

But there wasn't: the nearest ship deck was a cab ride and check-in away. The coords got mentally filed away in order, Lytaxin, Springwood, Tinsori Light. Well, that last one, that was one he'd been supposed to forget, to put out of his head as a last resort just ahead of, or maybe behind, Jumping into a sun. He'd not have had it at all except for the oddity of his grandmother knowing it, though she was not now and never had been a pilot.

Not dressed yet, Quin yos'Phelium Clan Korval stood in the cold of the near attic, falling into a dance routine to steady himself to gravity before he dressed. Surebleak's gravity was a bit light to his standards, not that the planet knew nor cared. Odd that he should still be dancing to the gravity of a world and school he'd been pulled from because of Plan B—but his small class at Trigrace was long graduated and he'd not be back there, probably ever.

There was a cat, briefly, a quick strop against his bare legs and away, regally.

"Silk," he called. "Silk?" He could use a moment of cat-time. . .

When calling the cat's name didn't halt the move toward the mystery space beneath the bookcase he made the silly Terran *catchacat-catchacat* sound this household preferred to the more sibilant Liaden *fizwisswisswiss...*

Cat eyes glowed at him momentarily from the cat-way, gave a slow, comforting blink, and then melted soundlessly into shadow.

"Tomorrow," he offered at the disappeared cat, and finished his stretches. His ring flashed in the morning light, reminding him he'd not chosen an earring yet. . .and that he was finally due for a quiet dinner with his father, the Boss.

#

It was Quin's rule never to leave his rooms without a gun–that had been the rule on the Rock, after all, to always go armed–and he'd not forgotten the memorable dust-up on the occasion of the recent All Boss party at Jelaza Kazone, where Cousin Theo'd showed Padi and him that, however good their training, they'd much to learn.

He'd been on the fringe of the action there–truthfully it was a good thing he'd not been in the middle of it else his martial failings would have surely been revealed to all.

But that action had been proof that things weren't settled here, so armed he and all the clan went.

Generally he had at least his gun, his backup, and knife. No one gainsaid him this–the clan was sure enough of him not to be concerned he'd misuse them and fond enough of him to permit what was hardly an ill-conceived notion on the chaotically burgeoning portside of Surebleak.

The guns were an added comfort for his familiarity with them, and the satisfaction he got from practice. He'd shot every other day when he was undertree and missed it dearly–both Nelirikk and Cheever McFarland applauded his skill, and he had no doubt that his last few impromptu matches there–he'd beaten both of them the last time–had been genuine. Nelirikk considered that he was the equal of his father with the pistol at distance. . .and that was good. He was also an excellent shot with a long arm, and improving on both.

He'd been set to shoot with his father and Natesa, perhaps a chance to test his skill against them both–but some necessity or another had always delayed that, and then he was called to the city, untimely.

Later this day was set a meal; he'd need be sure to be dressed for that as well. So he had worn two simple blue-gemmed bar cuffs, in case it meant a semi-formal event with his grandmother in attendance. She was stickler for detail. . .manners, cards, code, or clothes–she expected the best in all sides.

Checked, did he, on his protections then–glancing in the mirrors–and then looking to the infrared on the video to be sure that only the ornate public gun showed easily. It was an ostentation of a gun, in being only half-small and shiny, and on a trick-shot holster he'd won at Tey Dor's. Oddly, at Tey Dor's one would hardly ever wear such a thing–it was a holster meant for competition only. Here. . .

On Surebleak, there was such a thing as being over-subtle, a mistake the clan would not want made again. Showing no gun would be over-subtle. Showing this gun? A young person's fancy gun on a young person, who should be surprised? He knew his clan would forgive him since they knew it not to be his only protection. And this was the gun he'd matched shots even-up with Cheever. He would be forgiven for wearing it–it made him look in control.

In reality, control meant that he needed to recall that he was on Surebleak, and allow some play to his features, more than might be allowed on Liad–and that meant he had to feign a constant contentedness. He recalled the face that he'd practiced in the mirror, knowing his control was good.

So down to breakfast, reviewing his day's agenda. Besides attending a late-day discussion about Uncle Shan's possible relocation out of the port, his classroom piloting lessons–actually math lessons, without immediate reference to board or vids–were scheduled early. A Scout mentored him there, since his lacks were esoteric rather than generic. Lunch would be latish and he could walk from Griswold Plaza if he wanted, there being an opportunity to visit the rug and sock shop, or not, depending on time. Dinner–now that would be up to the Boss.

He sighed, considering the Boss, his father. Yes, Plan B had brought the family into open contention with their enemies, and Plan B had brought them here–here where his father, now the Boss, might insist that the proper study of a gentle born Liaden was the history of warring turfs, the balance of power between east side and west side, the weather–always the weather–and the details of neighborhoods and. . .

Well it was that the first thing he'd learned to study at Trigrace Eclectic was how to study, with classless independent study the norm and access to working scholars, and practical thinkers a requirement. Piloting, yes, he'd had that–something his father had never learned formally! He'd also had language study far beyond the usual Liaden range, and. . .well, since his early tests had shown he was neither destined for the Healer Halls nor the Scouts, he'd gone for Piloting as major, with a minor as Generalist. His father's studies had been more independent than that, of course. Despite being clan-bred, his father was very much a self-made man.

Quin, clan-bred as well, was a pilot now, but in the tradition of the clans he was expected to follow orders, which now meant he needed to prepare to be Boss. From what little he'd seen of his father since being ordered from Jelaza Kazone to the city, being a Boss had no reprieve, and little enough joy. His generalist background–well, that was useful–perhaps he could learn, or get by until he could escape to pilot.

#

The stairs he took were old and creaky. Near the dark spot at the bottom he slowed, whispering "Mistress Miranda" but not finding that ancient cat in the cubby-corner she'd adopted for busy mornings–close to the kitchen and dining room but away from the sometimes rushed comings and goings. Mistress was an old cat, and still grumpily recovering from her evacuation from his father's former home on Liad, where she'd rarely been beset by more than three or four visitors at once. At her Liad town home, too, she'd been the solo cat–and here, of course, there was already a resident feline.

Quin hoped she was curled comfortably somewhere. He could certainly sympathize with her problems–brought across space unexpectedly after a long separation from Pat Rin, to a strange house, only to find interlopers: both a new cat and a permanently ensconced human often occupying favored spots.

Breakfast staff had the small table reserved for Grandfather and him set, but it was obvious by lack of steaming cup that Luken was off again–likely at Ms. Audrey's, just as likely never home from last night.

Quin smiled, just a little. Grandfather's hints in that direction were growing stronger and Quin had been with him when Grandfather'd taken a call about the property across the street from Ms Audrey's front door. He might set up an annex there for the carpet center, was one thing. But there were extensive living quarters above the store front–which had been of much interest to Grandfather as well.

Breakfast for him came with two steaming cups–today's task was to name each beverage–so said the note with his tray. One was, thankfully, Morning's Fresh Blush Tea–and the other was much harder, it being a coffee. Like tea, coffee was said to have provenance. And like tea, coffee was said to have a perfect brewing time. He sighed, taking the dark drink without recourse to any available additives. Those things confused the palate as much for coffee as for tea–and he'd been trying to get used to dealing with his food and drink as he might find it visiting in any honest home on Surebleak, where additives might be too expensive, or too chancy, for the hosts.

He sighed again with the first sip. Not, then, what Cousin Miri would hold up as Merc Super–Merc Standard being a coffeetoot still worthy of two or three of the poorer food stands a distance from the Road, and Merc Super being what happened when a Merc cook dumped real ground coffee into a pot and kept it at near boil for a day or two, so as to always be ready for a needy troop.

He settled, after a third sip, on Lankshire Lakes Bold. That was a half-cheat, though, and it made him wonder. He'd seen the new packs arriving several days earlier. . .but no, that's what it was. Results and answers were required of him, not explanations about how he arrived at his conclusions.

His ride today was to be Mr. McFarland, a man who was as much a pilot as anyone on the planet, as far as Quin could figure, a man with amazing patience and. . .

. . .he ought to be having breakfast now, too.

That eight person "ready room" table where the Boss and his immediate hands often sat, was empty.

He looked again, analyzing. It wasn't merely devoid of people, it was devoid of–everything. No set-up, no cups, no utensils. It had been cleared then, and not set for a morning snack or lunch yet.

Too, there was no sign of Natesa–called Natesa the Assassin by some, and called Boss Natesa by others, and called Lifemate by his father. He sighed at that, for worse than the "natural lifemating" that happened to some in his clan, where the universe and genes conspired to make two people into one as with Delm Val Con and Delm Miri, this lifemating of Natesa and Pat Rin was a voluntary thing, born out of. . .born out of he did not know what. That they admired each other was sure. He'd heard one of the Surebleak hands say that they "deserved each other". . .and might be that was as good a reason they were together as any other.

Natesa had Boss duties of her own and so when the Boss was away she often sat solo at a table on the kitchen level above the half-stairs, like a cat with a perch of her own, overlooking the street through a gunslit converted to bulletproof window.

"You'll have more?"

Quin had heard the steps behind him, and recognized them, but he sat staring at McFarland's usual place at the empty table next to where his father often sat at morning council.

"Am I waiting for Mr. McFarland? He appears to have overslept."

"Nah, you know better, youngster. Overslept ain't like that man, and never was. That table's clear to supper or beyond. Cheever, he's with the Boss–the Port's decided to do their ship-station move early and they need all the pilots they have to. . ."

The coffee continued motion to his lips, the turn he'd begun to the cook's assistant never slowed. He nodded an acknowledgment of the news at her, his recent extra training at the knee of his grandmother serving him in good stead, his near smile still wedded to his face.

"Indeed? They needed pilots, did they? I wonder that I was not called. . ."

The assistant shrugged artlessly.

"Foo, Master Quin, how'd I know it? The messages come all in a rush while I was starting the bread oven to going; McFarland, the Boss, don't know who else called out. Oh, Ms. Natesa, she went. They'll let you know later, I'm sure–but might have been a Boss secret in it."

He finished his cup in a rush, which he knew better than to do, and looking into its depth he conceived a need to steady his face.

Him a pilot, and not called. His lessons, his plans all put aside. Clearly the duty-day schedule was wiped. . .

He fumbled for words, seething, his stomach fighting him momentarily, then a need to not move, for if he did get up now he'd run all the way to the tree. Best to stay here, in the seat, to pin himself to this place.

He covered the fumble with cough smothered in a napkin, followed by downing the last of his juice. He must not run!

Breath caught, he managed to gain time to think.

"More of this exact coffee, Jennetta, if I can, and yes, if I'm not on call, some of what's hot, sausages and spuds and rolls bashed with butter!"

"Why, that sounds like an honest breakfast for a change, don't it? It'll take a minute."

The servant dashed away, pleased, and he could hear her trading the news in the kitchen that "that boy's hungry today, without answering quiz-questions of the Boss and company for a change. . ."

Normally he'd be put out of humor to hear himself called "that boy," but he let it pass. He was practicing what Grandmother called appropriate restraint.

Grandmother. Well, yes, she and Grandfather had been firm while they were off on Runig's Rock–studies along with gun training, studies of card-games and card-skill, studies along with security work, studies along with ship-sitting. Studies. . .they'd had no moment for ruminations, that they had seen to.

He stared at but didn't see the table for some moments, memory returning to that haven, to the days when he had been the best pilot available and the clan's last hope if the enemy had come to them.

He went weak–he'd brought the ship out of there, he had, Runig's Rock under attack, Padi backing him up and. . .

And here he sat, while pilots were needed? What did they think, that he'd forgotten how to fly? What secret could be more precious than a cargo of the clan's last children? What. . .

But Grandmother had schooled him well, and to any observer still in the house his face was as unconcerned and uncomplicated as that of any simple day laborer on Wall-down duty.

"But here, Master Quin," came Jennetta's carrying voice well before her appearance from the kitchen, "there's a note left for you–for personal delivery at breakfast, the driver said."

She held it out for him with one hand, juggling a perilously filled bowl of rolls, a dish of butter, and a jam jar in the other before precariously bringing them successfully to table.

Dear Grandson, the note said in impeccable Liaden longhand. It was a familiar hand–not surprising, since Luken bel'Tarda, his grandfather, was quite fond of sending notes and letters and signed books–

Boss Conrad's business is quite pressing today and he has commandeered your driver and your pilot-mentor, and deputized myself and many others, likely for the whole of the day. I consulted with the Boss, who feels it is perhaps best for you to stay busy – and that rather than staying in house and being bored or joining me at Ms Audrey's, where I am involved with delicate negotiations, that you relocate for the day to The Emerald Casino and find occupation there. You will await the Boss, who will meet you there as time permits.

To call upon the casino for refreshments or a private parlor, merely show your dragon pin and say your name, and they'll have a scanner that will read your credentials.

You'll find Jemie's Cab Service is awaiting a call from you at your earliest convenience.

Text and subtext—whatever the Boss was doing was important, too important to share with the inexperienced. Too important for a note even from the Boss—his grandfather'd taken the informant role upon himself. Yes, Grandfather was a kinder man than his father, and more alert in some ways, too.

Perhaps unwisely he chugged the not half-full cup of coffee.

Jannetta, alert as she returned with the rest of his food, rushed to refill his cup, face full of smiles.

"Oh, good, I'm so glad you like it. We have a lot of it, and the tea bin got damp when the sink backed up. You'll be set for weeks!"

He nodded absently at her, wishing he was alone, or maybe doing the perimeter tour on Runig's Rock, one more time.

This cup of coffee was hotter, so he sipped it, scanned the food. Yes, he'd eat his breakfast and take his time; no reason to upset the staff by being short with them. *They* were not the ones ignoring him, *they* were not the ones forgetting his place in the family, *they* were not the ones forgetting his role in the clan!

Yes, he'd wait for the Boss. . .they had a lot to talk about.

He was basically dressed well enough for a daytime casino visit on Surebleak, of that he felt certain. First, of course, he'd need to call the taxi, and then, of course, select his jacket–and perhaps better jewelry, too, if his father was going to meet him there. Oh, and surely he'd not need snow-lugs at the Emerald Casino, if he was going by taxi, so he'd wear some better boots–at least his grandfather or grandmother might notice that he was somewhat dressed for society.

Halfway up the stairs he knew what jacket he'd wear, and so, which boots.

***

Villy Butler threw the sticks across the polished table, wrist snap sharp and accurate. *Palaz Dwaygo* sticks tumbled together in what he'd been taught to call a bar-galaxy, the kind of jumble that produced good betting and plenty of room for mischance. This was setup ideal for a challenge match – if he'd been playing House against it–well–he would. Good practice.

Studying the lay he posted two plastic practice chips on the bet line. Being the *Stro Palaz,* he added a blue to his, then to defense, and continued.

The morning was good for playing against the house and for the house, there being very few patrons in the casino at all and none yet wandering his end of the main hall.

The basic card players–they were a constant, like the dicers and the endless staccatos at the robot machines, and might be found round the clock, betting on a better tomorrow. The sticks players, like the roulettiers, tended to come in with the flow of traffic to and from the port. A busy day on port usually was a good thing, with the buzz of voices and the buzz of action.

Today–the whole place felt muted. The low-key morning music found few bodies to bounce off, none to excite to dance rhythm, none to inspire to sing along, none to drop coins or call for chips. The Emerald's automatics took care of sound levels and air-moving these days. Maybe if he coughed a few times he could prime a little energy into the place.

It was the weather, of course–the weather was good and the port's long-awaited changeover to new systems and orientation had been started in the overnight, with the advent of the good weather.

The weather and the port noise together could have put him to sleep if he'd not been scheduled here, though the night had been light.

Villy smiled, though he'd taken a financial hit–his late date at Ms. Audrey's had called off the tumble at nearly the last minute. At least it had been nearly the last; he hadn't lit the candles or started the oil warming or set out all the toys. He was sorry to loose the cash but the pilot promised him a bonus for the next time, to make up for what he'd called "opportunity costs."

There'd be opportunity costs today, too, it looked like–with no action, there'd be no tips.

In front of him, the sticks. Villy pulled seven. . .and then there was a slip.

Frowning, he added a chip to each side. . .and became the other player in the hand. . .and. . .sensed something, perhaps a shadow, moving.

The shadow half behind him was a Liaden, silent, precise, watching. His boots were pilot boots, as Villy had learned. The jacket was a pilot's jacket. The gun was a little bright, but if he was a pilot he'd have more than one, for sure.

He looked too young for a Scout, though he might have been–Villy had trouble figuring Liaden ages, smooth-skinned and beardless as they were–but he wore a pilot's jacket and ear rings rich enough to be a pilot of some experience or note.

But the jacket, worn loose, showed a local shirt and hint of glitter near the throat and the hair was looser and longer than he'd expect.

That was mixed signals, it was, and Ms. Audrey warned staff to watch for mixed signals at the House and he guessed the same mattered here at his share job. Something might be up and worth watching careful.

He weighed the pilot's looks, realized that he was closing in on staring, though the seeing was good.

"Pilot," he said with one of the careful nodding bows he'd learned from Cheever McFarland. "Are you interested in a game?"

Villy got back so exact a copy of his bow, with a hint of the lookover he'd been guilty of, and he wondered if he was being mocked. The face showed a firmness he was becoming used to among the Liadens he dealt with; in fact it could be of the same mold as Boss Conrad or the Keeper of the Road. Alert blue eyes reading his moves and face while giving back little enough. There was, maybe, a very little hint of an ironic smile. It made him feel, that look did, as if the observer had an advantage, and knew it, or had seen him looking a trifle long. The Boss himself had a look like that.

Still, Villy had experience looking at men; this one was interesting, nearly tempting. Perhaps there was advantage on two sides if they should play a throw or two.

"A game?" The voice was polished, with that Liaden lilt, and Villy held his sigh back. Perfect, even spoken in Terran with the slightest edge of a Surebleak click.

"Perhaps I will game later, but not immediately, no. I meant not to distract you, but rather to watch your practice."

"Watching a game as you participate is a wonderful way to learn," Villy offered, seeing the suppressed grin flit across the pilot's comely golden face. "Are you familiar with the game?"

Villy swept the practice sticks up, half-looking to the pilot, and was startled when the jumble revealed an escaping blue, which he let go rather than risk the bundle. The blue was snapped out of the air by the pilot well before it reached the floor.

In a single motion the stick was returned to him with a bow of some complexity.

"Indeed, V. Butler, I have some experience of it. It was wise of you not to attempt that recovery."

V. Butler–Ah, his name badge. Pilots were sharp ...

"I'm Villy Butler. And for this game, I am *Stro Palaz*, you know, Game Master, for the morning. To keep that, I gotta practice. This is a practice tube – for the games, we have *Palaz Dwaygo* Solcintra-style, with the standard thirty-six, with colors; else we have the local Quick-sticks, same length but light weight, twenty-five plus the pick-stick. The other tubes are sealed, and. . ."

"The Boss offers choice. I should have known."

"Of course the Boss offers choice! Why, the. . ."

But that quick the pilot's hand rose in sign Villy almost knew, and he said, "Peace, Villy Butler. If the Boss says it, so must it be, eh?"

Villy held his retort back, offering now a tube of each sort.

Again a mystery bow, this time with a bit more of a smile.

"Perhaps when there's more action, my friend, if I am here that long. I'm..."

Here it was as if the pilot was at a sudden standstill for words, as if his Terran had failed him. He went on–

"I'm to meet someone here," he said, "regarding occupation."

Then he shrugged, adding, "They could not tell me when they will arrive with any precision, other than today. I am, so to speak, at their convenience, as time permits. So, let me explore–the last time I was here there was no time to acquaint myself with the facilities–and perhaps I'll play if I have time."

Villy accepted a kind of half-bow, collecting the sticks carefully while watching the pilot move on, steps coordinated and silent. Well then, the morning wasn't half-wasted, after all. Practice, with a view.

***

Quin ambled away from the comely young Game Master, by habit acquainting and reacquainting himself with obvious exits, likely exits, and potential exits, as well as the permanent staff stations, the rest rooms, the doors to the private parlors. Off to one side, he knew, was the private room where staff had "held" the delm on their first visit. As if *they'd* be "held" by anything as flimsy as the port's *real* whosegow, much less a room with a lock on the plastic door.

The casino was remarkably devoid of patrons this morning, a mere dozen or so scattered throughout.

A careful appraisal revealed nearly as many visible staff as customers, which was well enough, for it permitted him a good look at the results of the recent upgrade. The lighting was more subdued than the last time he'd seen it; the seating improved, the flooring more resilient and sound absorbing. He'd heard discussions of the aromatics, mood lights, and sounds supplied by a *nerligig* sitting in a re-purposed closet–as the room filled, the music and scents would strengthen and the lighting would become more focused on the equipment, allowing patrons the feeling that they were not cram-full and reinforcing the reason they were there–to gamble.

Quin received nods of apparent recognition from several of the staff, as well as a few customers. A passing Scout accorded him a cordial bow, and he got two profuse pairs of bows from elderly Liaden gallants in last year's Solcintran afternoon wear.

The two gallants, now. He'd seen them, elsewhere, together. The first image came to him as he demanded it. Yes, the memory games Grandmother had taught on station were working! His saw the gallants now in his head, more than their faces, distantly sipping from crystal glasses at Trealla Fantrol, politely bowing to Uncle Shan. He. . .he must have barely been in public then.

Emigres, then, distant allies of Korval, coming to one of the few places on Surebleak with even a remotely Liaden tang to it.

Quin paused, wondering how many other such there were now on world, and how many arriving, wondering what more they could do here but stand in the wake of pilots. Here there were no Liaden clubs, no Tey Dor's to shoot and be seen at, no promenade, no. . .

Truth, he missed Tey Dor's himself, as rarely as he'd been there–so many stories of his clan echoed there, so many stories of yos'Phelium. . .so many of his father. He missed it not only because of the utility of practice and competition, but for the society of it.

He moved on, completing his tour. There wasn't much more to see. The Emerald might be the best casino on planet, but it was still a smaller operation than one would find on most port city peripheries elsewhere in the galaxy.

He sighed as he stood in front of a row of the robot bet-offs, having no pressing interest there. On the other hand, several of the card tables were peopled, and he moved into observe. . .

Alas, the occupied tables backed on a closed section, there being no need to spread out. Ah, well, no close up spectating this way, which was a shame. Quin looked about him. The wheels now. . .the gambling wheels usually permitted. . .

His scan took in the back of the room, where V. Butler was earnestly practicing the sticks.

A glance to the chronometer over the service counter showed him. . .that the clock was artfully sited to receive as much glare as possible, and thus was difficult to read.

He flipped his hand through several iterations of the pilot sign *no details yet* to himself. He took three steps forward, and now the clock was visible, but no real help.

The clock told him nothing: as ever, he didn't know when his father would arrive. He didn't know what was to be discussed. He didn't know. . .

The same often maintained at his new home: the Boss would arrive when he did, unless he'd stayed in working in his office, which he often did; sometimes he'd be held from dinner or lunch, of breakfast by some or another strangeness, sometimes he'd come to table a few minutes after his Natesa arrived and sometimes with her—and no time, either for Quin, no matter that he'd been warned to expect real duty, any day now. He'd been told the move from undertree was to train him to be Boss. To be Boss!

So here he stood while the real work of the Boss was going on within view of the front door.

Quin grimaced, ruefully pleased that Grandmother wasn't there to see him with his face so open. A pilot's quick relaxation exercise brought him some calm, but still –

What he *should do* was flash his Tree-and-Dragon, demand a quiet place to sit, and study. There were still unfinished lesson modules from TriGrace he could access, and there was always piloting math to ...

He felt the anger rising again, then.

No.

His father had sent him here. Or his father and Natesa. Or the Boss and his grandfather. They'd *sent him here* while there was work to be done, *piloting work*. . .and they'd sent him to the Emerald. For occupation.

Very well then. If he was to wait at the Emerald and be occupied there, if he was to wait "as time permits," he would damn well *be* occupied.

Oh yes, he would.

#

He made a desultory run at a console card sim picked randomly; it burbled game choices until he stabbed the button rapidly to change languages, annoyed by thing's terribly accented Trade. The hands were fast, but his coin was multiplied several times, and he challenged the machine to games and to languages, making it speak to him in homeworld Terran, and then in what it thought was Looper Terran, just for the practice.

Someone else was playing nearby, and apparently losing, for he heard what might have been the slam of disappointed hand on console.

His public pocket had been nearly to let when he'd started–in his sudden preparations he hadn't bothered to arm himself with Terran bits above what he normally carried. Now he had a game card. . .which he stuffed into that pocket, starting another. He'd heard a machine on the other side of the aisle make the *player out of funds* sound, and someone sighed, loudly.

The console card game was flat, though he was winning. Despite his practice of two calming mental exercises he still felt an undercurrent of tension which he couldn't resolve–and it didn't help that the casino was hardly soundproof, so the action at the spaceport rumbled through from time to time. He stood up straighter, remembering that he was a pilot, dammit, and not a school child, and moved down the aisle, waiting on the pleasure of his elders and stalking opportunity here.

He walked, cringing at some of the front panels, and moved by a machine calling itself *Target Practice* as numbers on a multiplier panel jumped from two to seven. There, the promise of an extra seven times payout–why not? It was denominated in half bits, which amused, and so he stopped to play.

Given the images of weapons, he chose the personal models, and then the rarities...

The machine took a fair portion of his earnings quickly, but he played with the choices of caliber, style, and targets. On the fifth run he threw his hand-arm against a longshot, and was rewarded with a slowly rising whoop of machine joy, which gave way to. . .*oh*! He'd hit that shot, at seven times the stake, with a red bonus. The bonus matched his original stake and–on screen–appeared as piles of energy packs. The multiplier was still in effect and the totals kept rising and voices announced he was into triple bonus round. He'd already won quite a bit–wouldn't his father be amused to discover he'd come away with a cantra? There was some amount of money in reserve, he wouldn't know how much until the next round.

Now he had to choose his weapons again.

He laughed, chose a silly looking zero-gravity dueling pistol, and touched the machine to urge it on. Targets began to arise.

Someone was standing close by, and then started playing the game next to his. Ah, searching for the lucky spot, no doubt. Well. No matter.

His machine blinked and brightened–now the multiplier was showing an even dozen!

Quin laughed again, for there were a dozen targets to chose from on the machine, all valuable gems on distant pedestals. Well, all gems but for the gaudy necklace of pearled firegems with a firegem pendant–so he chose that, and palmed the trigger button.

The machine's antics were amusing as the pistol lined up on screen and a single bullet entered the firing chamber through a ghostly hand. Then it asked hm to choose windage and loft and if the pistol pulled high or to the right or. . .

His choices were random, and he pressed the shoot button.

The machine dutifully mimicked a supposed shooting sound and showed his shot traveling. . .arcing very neatly to hit the blazing firegem pendant full on.

The firegem spun in its virtual spot, spitting fire! Dancing from the flames were numbers, and each number accompanied by a beep, or a horn, or the flash of light or color, and sometimes all. . .

It was amazing, and then appalling.

Quin took a half-step back as the sound continued and numbers ran, all in bits. He translated as best he could to the latest approximation in cantra as the numbers ran on. . .and then halted.

Had it actually come to a cantra? Well, more or less, since the exchange rate varied. Still . . .maybe more than a cantra!

Quin saw the screen reform into a fire-rimmed challenge:

"Double or Nothing, sharpshooter?" it asked.

It took no time to decide *that* question.

Quin cashed out, waiting patiently for the card to clear, then holding it in hand a moment.

Around him now, others—staring at the machine. A casino employee came by, nodded brusquely.

"Done with this session, sir?"

"I am," Quin bowed, stuffing the chit into his public pocket with the other.

"Need security?"

It was not a silly question on a world like Surebleak, and if he'd needed a ride to quarters he'd not have been behind with the request. . .

"I do not."

"My turn," a Terran voice demanded, but the security man said, "Hold, friend," and waved a portable read-wand at the machine. "We have to take records of the major wins, you know. Just a moment."

The machine blinked, chattered, rebooted into brightness—and the multiplier lights fell from 12 to 1.2.

The man beside him made noises—a local by the hard-worn looks of him—and he stared at the machine, a low continuous stream of cussing going on.

"My run," he was muttering, "shoulda been my run!"

#

Quin stood, surveying the rest of the casino distantly. Not another robot game at this point, especially not with the burly Terran already busy shoving funds into *Target Practice*. . .

Well. The cards were in progress, but perhaps not those, either–he'd chosen the robogames because leaving would be easy, when the Boss arrived.

The sticks–Villy seemed a pleasant enough table host. That was an idea now that he had enough cash to buy a bundle or two. By now there might be a game there–or he could start one.

His steps led that way, and there was Villy, packing his practice sticks away one by one. At tableside was a Terran as badly dressed as the one he'd just left behind, hulking, and apparently waiting.

The sticksman now was presenting two tubes to the newcomer, who was larger even than Mr. McFarland, very pale, and extravagantly overdressed unless one had never before been challenged to meet the mere freezing point of water.

Quin moved forward, hand motioning his desire to buy in.

* * *

The pretty pilot was back, which was a relief. The *'reesta*, meanwhile, was either a fool or a fraud; could anyone really be that unaware of the way things worked in a casino after having been in the Emerald hours at a time these past five days? Well, Villy'd never had him at *this* station, but he had seen him and his crony about, hanging at the low robots for long stretches and sometimes drifting to the cheap cards. It was hard to miss men so unused to Surebleak's weather, or so willing to play the cheap games.

And so Villy'd explained that if the man played *him* at the base rate that he, Villy, would represent the House directly. . .yet the man was still confused about the difference between the casino, the House, Villy and...

The pilot arrived, looked to the man and then to Villy–

"Has a bundle been purchased? Is there a game building? May I join?"

"No decision there, pilot, while deciding's going on," Villy managed respectfully, adding, "would you like to consult over choices? Would you care to challenge or be challenged?"

Villy hopefully held a tube of each kind toward the pilot, who bowed acknowledgment and turned to the over-dressed newcomer.

"Surely anyone can see that the Solcintran style is superior for the player of quality and experience. The extra sticks make the game more difficult, and played for color, there's considerable complexity! The Quick-sticks are light fare. They are perhaps adequate for someone passing time on the port while expecting a flight, or waiting to be joined by a companion."

Villy absorbed these words, offered in Terran, and held them to him: the pilot was young, not much older than Villy himself–despite which he was a man with good sense and excellent understanding. These words, repeated wisely, were worth bits in Villy's pocket in the future, surely.

"Obviously you see yourself as superior with the *Liaden-style*," the tourist said accusingly–Villy thought of him as The Coat, for the purple and red-striped garment he wore–"but I'm willing to play a game and try them out. Name low stakes, sir, and I'll try your choice."

The pilot slid his hand into his public pocket and pulled out a handful of Terran change, looking to Villy with a slight smile.

"Let me see what I carry sir–perhaps I'll have my lunch money made into chips. I suppose we should start low, to find a range."

"Lunch money? Hah! They feed you here, if you win!"

"As luck favors," the pilot murmured. He nodded to Villy and stepped away, toward the bank.

#

The pilot was as good as his word, returning to buy the first bundle with a five pale chip and offering his opponent, "Five pales to start, if you like, for the first game."

Villy had quick eyes–the five pales the pilot offered were matched by one in his hand. Villy worried briefly–perhaps the ten *had been* all the money the pilot owned?

The other player laughed; it was an ugly sound compared to the pilot's voice, and it faded into an ugly smile filled with ugly, multi-colored teeth. His coat stank of smoke and a hint of old *vaya* and sweat, and the striped sleeves waved gracelessly and then fluttered as he moved his meaty hands in emphasis.

"Sure, why not get our fingers warmed up before we throw money at Lady Luck?"

Villy looked around but saw no such lady. Lucks–formal, paid Lucks that is, people whose mere presence was said to change fortune for others–were specifically not permitted at the Emerald. The rule was clearly posted!

The pilot bowed, acknowledging a witticism, also bowed to the, "I'll buy the second tube," which was only fair.

"Shall you twist, or shall I?"

The pilot thus offered choice of first throw–but that was a Solcintran habit, Villy'd learned–and twisted the tube with a sharp snap, breaking the seal as his opponent waved him to it.

With the game joined, Villy stepped back.

Like the man's voice, the throw was ugly. The table strike was awkward, with sticks bouncing rather than spreading naturally, and the clicks of the late-falls were ragged rather than rhythmic. Villy held his face close, but not as close as the pilot, who might have not seen anything amiss but the blandness. Meanwhile The Coat nodded and smiled, as if everything was exactly like he wanted it.

At this juncture, Villy's job was as spotter—with the aid of the back-up camera of course, if anybody called foul.

He watched carefully as The Coat's first three lifts went well. His technique seemed to require small motions over tortuous amounts of time, and both squinting and special breathing, not to mention craning his neck for the best view angle. Despite the second lift—using a dangerous leverage technique—he seemed in control. The fourth—no need for a camera there—the bobble was significant, clearly moving three other sticks and quickly admitted with an under-voiced curse.

The pilot. . .was completely at ease as his turn started, in fact so at ease that he appeared to have no technique at all to his pickups—no special breaths, no extreme staring or checking of angles, and Villy sighed when the rest of that pile was done at about the time The Coat was muttering, "Remarkable!"

The pilot nodded, glanced into the large man's face and offered, "Another then, at the same rates, to see if Lady Luck walks by?"

#

The pilot, having collected his fifth straight round-up, sighed gently. The Coat had been becoming louder, and twice had asked for screen-checks of pick-ups that were flawless. He'd insisted on doubling the bets after the third course, and had taken a moment's break for some sort of meditative breathwork Villy didn't recognize. Even after the break his attempts were growing less fluid, and taking absurdly long–in fact, the pilot might have called foul, so long had one taken.

Villy was beginning to worry. The pilot was. . .very good, and Villy was supposed to watch out for pros, or for Sharps, roving gamblers looking for the less skilled to fleece. He hoped the pilot wasn't a Sharp–in fact if he wasn't losing so bad he'd have taken The Coat for a Sharp on actions alone. . .

The pilot's left hand held the sticks and he gently tapped the ends into his free right palm.

"The matter seems not to be one of dispute, sir. The game is hardly a gamble for me unless we go to handicaps, and I'm not one to play. . ."

Villy breathed a little easier–maybe the pilot was *not* a roving gambler in search of a victim but a man looking for some relaxation and play. . .

"Wait, no, if you really were playing your lunch money, now you're playing with *my* money. I'll buy a new tube and we'll play at real rates–and we'll have a coin flip to decide which style tube! I see how you play, like it means nothing to you. Stopping now means you've tugged me wrong! You've put me on!"

Villy stepped forward, the rising animosity in The Coat's demeanor concerning.

"Sir, your opponent has suggested that more play would be unfair to you. I think that's a sign that. . ."

The pilot reached into his public pocket, showing his winnings.

"These few chips mean I've tugged you wrong? I think you do not know what it is to be tugged wrong, sir. But so, we'll play on, if you insist. I promise to concentrate, if that will permit you to concentrate."

Villy grimaced. The Coat seemed not to take the same sense from that last bit that Villy did. . .Still there'd been discussion and agreement, and not an argument. That was good, he thought.

***

Quin ran the pilot's rainbow as the sticks came to his hand, and his throw was good: there was a complex stack to work with, and the bottom of the pile richer than the top. The purple crossed the blue under the red – good point value there.

"Thus we'll play for twenty-five pales plus five up for each color up the rungs?"

The Coat looked at the pile and nodded, "Your call. I now reserve to match for any runs of over one hundred."

The pilot bowed, the minor tic of a smile at one corner of his mouth, and glanced around before giving an almost Terran shrug and taking position.

***

Villy had noticed already what the pilot saw: several passersby had become witness and audience, and another was moving closer. There seemed to be more people in the Emerald now, some of them workmen he recognized from frequent lunchtime play, one he knew as a functionary recently added to the port roster; a sometime client of his, from Audrey's. He'd be the third in the gallery. . .

The sound of the sticks absently tapped on end before the throw brought his eyes to the table, and there, the flash of color, and an admirable spread.

Villy settled back to watch, and indeed, the pilot did seem more intent now. His concentration had improved, his hand-motions were more precise. He was also, Villy thought, he was purposefully–yes. There it was. There was a delay that Villy measured as *one two three four, one two three four*, between pickups. If it was designed to distract, annoy, or to aid concentration, he couldn't guess.

In any case, the throw was run, and the pilot, intent, looked into the eyes of his opponent, who had remained silent.

"Shall I continue? Same?"

The chips moved, and it was so–the pilot went on. The tube was run again and once more. . .

The pilot looked up, first at Villy, then at The Coat.

Without hesitation he continued to pick up as he spoke. . .

"When I finish this run, you'll have a match of two hundred sticks. That will suffice for me. When your run is over, I'll break for lunch."

The run continued, smoothly, and just shy of mechanically. The cadence continued, and colors and angle were of no moment as those smooth hands worked.

Indeed, the pilot picked up his two hundredth stick, and then the five remaining on table he rolled under his hand carelessly, on purpose.

"Yours!"

That was awful familiar–that show of self-assured arrogance. In fact, Villy thought he'd once–only once!–seen Boss Conrad do the same thing, right at this table. He did it to a guy who'd been bad-mouthing the Emerald as a back-water bar, and the Boss had shown the guy exactly the way the game was played, taking him down five rounds in a row.

Villy smiled at that. The Boss was busy these days and he didn't get to see him often.

But at the table now, The Coat was sweating, and seething.

"Ruin a run to show off? You'll destroy your luck for sure! I've got you now!"

There was a murmur from the onlookers. . .

The audience was grown to nearly a dozen, two-thirds of them native Terran, a reasonable gallery for a busy day, but for this one, it meant other parts of the casino were empty because they were watching the show here.

He'd hear from the floor boss about that–he should have by now called for the drink-dancer. Easy enough, he touched the collar stud to call her. Someone besides the pilot ought to be making money. . .

"These have been working," The Coat said to Villy– "and now they owe revenge. We'll continue!"

The crowd grew closer and thicker and the sticks chittered when they were thrown. The Coat was hanging close to them now, muttering, staring, measuring with hand motions, leading his moves with dips of the shoulder, but moving more rapidly, also, as if he'd learned some lesson from the pilot's measured movements.

Around them whispered bets for and against The Coat, Liadens offering more against The Coat than for, their odds in dozens while the Terrans did tens and fifties.

Oblivious, The Coat ran three tubes flawlessly and there were payouts in the crowd for passing the hundred, for passing the third tube, for. . .

Then a very difficult lay, with several balance points at risk. The crowd hushed, and Villy's eyes went to the camera views for close up.

On another day he might have thought he saw a movement, but if he did the pilot's eyes nor the crowd's had seen it, and the play went forward. The next two pickups were easier, and the—

The slip this time was perceptible to all, and led to a slow cataclysm of rolling, sliding sticks. The watchers watched, began to mumble, mutter, or laugh depending on their stakes in the matter, and the Terran seemed to deflate within his coat, the color going out of his face.

The pilot bowed then, first to Villy, and then to The Coat.

"Your time is up, sir. My play at the sticks is done for the day..."

The pilot's bow and meaning was unmistakable.

"But wait—you have to give me a chance to..."

Several others were coming forward as if to fill the void left by the pilot. The Coat's face was red, and he turned, one hand going out as if to reach for the pilot. Villy turned his back to the large man and gestured with his hands to the crowd, effectively thwarting the move.

"The tube's run," Villy announced with as much gravity as he could muster, "And," he said, very loudly, "this is my mandatory coffee break!"

That was enough to bring the nearest marked security sliding in from opposite sides of the room—"mandatory coffee break" being the week's code words for potential problem customer—but by then the crowd was in motion, many following the pilot toward his next station.

"Coffee break!" roared The Coat into the rapidly thinning crowd, "I'll tell you what. You owe me for breaking my chance here. It was *my turn* to win. Let me play you! I want your game!"

"Coffee break," Villy insisted. "I can't!"

"Look," The Coat said to approaching team, pointing toward Villy, "This guy ought to be playing me now! He owes me a shot to get my money back!"

Villy ignored the man, gathering the tubes into their lockbin and ostentatiously turning the key over to the uniforms.

"Coffee break," security insisted mercilessly, "Play continues later."

* * *

Quin took several steps away, then turned, meaning to tip the Game Master, but that worthy was already chatting profusely with Security and heading off to one of the backrooms. The man who'd had too much money stood staring after him.

Quin sighed – that was a connection he wanted to sever. Coffee break meant that Villy Butler would be back at his station eventually and Quin could tip him later. Quin offered himself a pilot's loose *return at will* hand-motion and –

He hesitated, thinking to take a brief break among the robots, and perhaps have a snack. . .

Who *were* these people? Somehow he'd gained a cometary tail of gamblers and followers, something he hadn't expected. Seeing he'd paused, with neither bowing nor intro the following Terrans started in ...

"Pilot, good hands there!"

"Luck's with you–saw you at the spinners!"

"Oh, don't run–play's better here than that–he's a fluke and a hanger–saw him here yesternight begging play with his betters."

The locals, there were at least two, judging by accent, were less flattering.

"Shouldna wasted nowits time, and poor Villy outta the play, too, and dem chisletoes got the fingers of a branch-bumbling charcoal grubber."

Quin suppressed a grin on that one. That was close enough to calling the man a lackwitted fool as to make no matter–if the man only heard it to know it.

Uncomfortably close to his side now was someone he'd noticed before–one of the gallants unofficially attending the Scout. It struck him that the Scout, like him, spoke Liaden, and that the gallants might after all be lonely for the sound of home, in a place where Liaden was heard, but was hardly universal, and where etiquette sometimes meant stepping aside quickly to the implied demand of, "Coming through!"

A bow, and a murmured comment from that gallant.

"Pilot, your *melant'i* shows very well there. Continued play would be an affront to anyone of skill or breeding."

"Yes," Quin agreed, probably rather short, and his bow of acknowledgment even shorter. He desperately wracked his brain for the gallant's name or clan, but lacking–well, they were not on Liad, and he could walk on.

Two Terrans intercepted him now–

"Pilot, are you up to *our* challenge? Will you return to the sticks after the coffee break?"

The gallant began to say something more, but another Terran arrived, "Please, join me in a game. I'm sure that I'll offer more play and. . ."

The cometary tail had become a group, and he bowed a *no, thank you*, which was lost among the unseemly Terran waving and the voices.

"I am done with sticks for today," he said. "Clearly there's no competition."

"No competition? How can you say. . ."

Exasperated, Quin fought the Terran/Liaden/Trade interface, finally summing up with a rush.

"I have done sticks and am not beaten. I came to meet someone, and that is what I will do."

The noise continued, and one near his elbow was asking. . .

He raised his voice again, to reach the challengers at the far side who were calling out to him, "Pilot, you must play. Luck's running you but I can beat you!"

"Quiet! This is not luck. It appears I can beat anyone in the casino at will and. . ."

The buzz about him had fallen silent at his command, and now the entire room was watching him. The hidden *nerligig* amplified the silence, and then the rhythm of his words, producing new music, with power.

The gallant at his side was twittering over something, and the purposeful march of a leather-coated figure split his field of vision.

"Pilot," said the Scout he'd seen before, "You impugn all of us as lacksters and amateurs with such an attitude. I'll grant you the sticks–they're of little matter. Now, best of five at any station, or until you're out of funds, if you dare."

He had, of course, meant any challenge at sticks. He'd not meant to take on the casino. But this, this. . .

He laughed, allowing a smile to remain on his face. *If I dare!*

"Of course *I dare*," he said, "at any station you name. Until you give up, or until necessity calls me away. I await occupation."

She looked him up and down, took in his boots, and then his public gun.

"*At will,* pilot, is what you said. Best of five. How about piket?"
"Piket? Fine. That will be occupation enough."

***

Villy watched on the monitors while he ate and sipped coffee, hoping that the pilot hadn't fled after the rudeness at the sticks board–but he'd said he'd come to meet someone, and as far as Villy could tell, he hadn't yet. Sounded like the pilot was looking for a job. The casino was often used as a meet spot these days, the local restaurants and rooming houses weren't nearly up to the style some of the newcomers preferred. Ms. Audrey was even renting out parlors to some of the larger job searchers during the day, and had cut down on the perfumes in them since Liadens preferred rooms not quite so fancy smelling.

The pilot though, he'd gone off in a hurry. Maybe he had been risking all his blunt and need to count up before coming back to the fray. . .

In fact, there he was, which relieved Villy greatly. He and Scout dea'Liss were at piket with two side players, and whatever crowd the Emerald had were mostly assembled to watch. Hardly found that stuff in the daytimes, but a good crowd was worth money later, when everyone broke to play or challenge. . .

Villy grabbed a last sip of his coffee–one of the perks of the job was as much coffee as you wanted–and stood, catching camera fourteen's angle.

It was a good close up of his pilot, a good one. Serious face, strong more than cute, good ears and chin–and Liaden, which Villy was coming to appreciate greatly, since among other things beard burns were a real issue for someone in his regular line of work.

Well, his loss again. He wasn't allowed to pass a business card or referral for Ms. Audrey's when he was on duty here, not less he was directly asked. And the pilot hadn't asked. Good gambler–concentrated, had firm fine hands and a steady eye.

He flashed his thumbs over the reader and took a deep breath. Villy Butler, back on duty. Just an hour more and the rest of the day was his.

* * *

There were distractions Quin hadn't counted on, ranging from the smell of food–he turned down several trays on his way to the table, wanting only to get on with this challenge–to the motions and small sounds of the other patrons. The music and the other background sounds provided by the closeted nerligig helped. The establishment was using not Tey Dor's hallowed and time-tested undersounds, meant for refined Liaden gentlemen, but a rough mix meant to give patrons some small relief from the bustle of the port.

Nor was the Scout unaccomplished. Her game was considered, her demeanor flawless, and her gallants far more nervous than she. It was a good thing, he decided, that they watched from behind her–he'd hate to be concerned over double watching while playing someone with real skill. He was slightly amused by their choice of beverage and wondered if it was economy or curiosity which drove them to drinking the local beer. But there, if they were transplants of reduced means, they might yet need develop that taste–some of immigrants from Solcintra had come with their luggage, their names, and nothing more.

As was, the cards were keeping most of his attention; for the third hand in a row he was being forced to play defensively. He had experience there–at Runig's Rock they'd played hand after hand of piket while waiting for news that Plan B was over. Grandfather and grandmother were both resourceful players, and they told his mistakes over and again, not out of vanity but out of necessity. Who knew but that he'd have to take up his father's occupation when this was over? Who knew then, but that he'd be *the* yos'Phelium?

So far, none of the hands had gotten exorbitant, he had held off her rather obvious first hand attempt at a Clan Royale though it meant having to settle for barely above even Dozen's Lot in the first, she discarding judiciously to avoid either a Scout's Progress or a Triple Flash and thus taking that hand on a simple extra seven.

This hand was looking much like the last. He barely registered the added sounds of shoes and boots until it too went to an extra seven–this in his favor.

"Two hands to one," she said as the cards went to her, "you play well for a pilot with a such a new jacket. . ."

He failed to rise to the bait, though some of the crowd chuckled, and he saw there were indeed more than before, and wished they'd thought to call for a private parlor. There were Scouts and other pilots in the group, some back with handwiches, and before the deal two more tables got underway.

He glanced quickly about–perhaps the port work was done?

No sign, yet, of his father, and none either of Mr. McFarland or Natesa the Assassin. There was, he saw, Villy Butler, now in a flattering coat and wearing no name badge, on the edge of the crowd, a spectator. Yes, there were more folks about, so the shifts were changing, and there'd be more people still if he recalled schedules right.

Quin looked to his resources, wondered if perhaps he'd been being too conservative. He ought to have come out far ahead so far, two hands up, he ought to have been more active. The blush of challenge was worn well away now, he could tell, and he felt the edge that he'd had in the first game and that serenity in the second had fled. A pilot's relaxation drill then, and the hand came to him.

He settled in, and the hand became a disaster in short order, the cards falling into something he'd be lucky to force into a Small Cluster or a Nebularity to keep her away from. . .the ship sounds from outside had faded and the sounds of boots and mumbling around. He heard a whispered voice, "That pilot said he can beat anyone in the casino at will. . ."

The whisper was shushed about then, his glance showing Villy Butler in the area, still. Quin took up his cards, looked into them, and knew he'd be hard put to name a worse hand to hold at this juncture.

The Scout's expression was almost apologetic as she quickly laid down the cards of an Arch Flush, all blue. "Mine," she said, "pilot."

"Even," he said, acknowledging the lost hand with a bow so bare it was a nod, "the cards bled blue."

So his shuffle, and a scrape of boot against a chair, of chair against table, and he looked up to see Mr. McFarland's acknowledging blink and guided glance.

There, Natesa, her face wearing an appraising look he'd not seen on her before. If she acknowledged him, it was only by not looking away.

Out of sight, or perhaps not yet arrived, was The Boss.

He felt himself blush, felt the tension rising in him. He'd waited for hours. He'd dealt with a rude Terran, and now, *now* that he had occupation, they came to stand on the edge of things and stare at him.

McFarland. McFarland's eyes were oh so lazy at times; but his face held more than a Liaden's would, and hidden among the shadows of nose and chin was a slight smile.

Well. That was something. . .

The cards were called and as he got them to deal Quin looked up.

His father was paused near the two gallants, face blander than a new 'crete walk, making small bows of acknowledgment to them. He wore the on-duty smile required of a mixed patron establishment but was making his way across the room slowly, his shiny near-new pilots jacket even more old-style than the Liaden finery the gallants wore.

The cards went out, in proper order, but they were nearly unattended by Quin, who found and then denied the relaxation exercise that presented itself. He'd felt out of breath and closed in, but as he lifted his cards and fanned them, it was as if the cards were closer and the color more intense than they'd ever been—as if the cards were there for him.

He must fly the cards as if he were at a ship's board. He would not acknowledge his father until play was through.

Again the necessity to glance up—and his father was not apparent—off to his office, most likely; Mr. McFarland and Natesa both leaned, listening, each to their own of the elder Solcintran pair.

The hand was built; it held several opportunities and he threw negligent chips to the pile, doubling his usual opening bet. He'd never played a serious game before his father's eyes, so now he leaned on the assorted wisdoms of those who had trained his father, and saw only the cards and the table; barely even glancing at his opponent but to measure her glances between chips and cards, between one end of her hand and the other.

The Scout may have said something mild when he added more freight to the chips; his bow saw her match, and add more. They evened the pile several times, and her glance between cards and pile grew longer as she matched again.

The hand held two possibles now, and it was his chance to challenge, *if he dared.*

"Luken would play this, aiming to cash in at the long range, a slow game, but surer," his grandmother seemed to say in his ears, "and I would play this, to complicate and force. The challenge tests the will rather than the cards."

They had not played this hand exactly, at Runig's Rock, but a mirror of it. Quin did the math and the cards were smooth as Silk's fur in his hands, and the Scout's small joke about his jacket came back to him. Yes, new and fresh, was it?

He showed a card that drew two, he showed another and it drew. The colors were running in his favor, but there was risk.

His turn now to challenge–"Will you double if I do?"

He held the chips in hand, and the Scout pursed her mouth, wrinkled her nose the way a Terran might when sniffing coffee in the morning.

"Pilot, I believe I will sue for the next hand."

There! She dropped her hand and waved her chips toward him. She said with a bow, "Your choice of a slow win or a fast, once your cards fall. Elegant enough, I need not see the demonstration."

#

The next hand then: no pause for a handwich, nothing but a sip of water for him. The Scout was drinking strong tea; and had taken a quick closed eyed stretch. None of that for him; what he did was to locate the towering figure of Mr. McFarland, who stood now behind the two gallants, watching over Natesa, the lifemate of Pat Rin yos'Phelium. Natesa, whose judge's eyes showed nothing to him at all when their glance crossed, other than she watched.

His father, the Boss, was still not in evidence at the moment.

Indeed. The casino's owner, after all, should not be playing favorites, and had work to do, besides.

Tension in has hands, tension also rose in Quin's stomach. Not much chance of the Boss playing favorites, eh? The casino's owner clearly had his priorities set, and a son not the most convenient among them.

The crowd now consisted of pilots and Scouts and local workers, too, with a smattering of Liadens like the gentlemen who'd be trailing the Scout so eagerly before times. Up in the crowd Quin saw some of the other non-locals–including his late opponent, standing just a step or two away from and behind Villy.

His problem, he was reminded, was the cards coming to him now; his problem, was winning.

The cards went face down before him. Quin put his hands on them, closed his eyes briefly, and before looking at them at all pushed the previous game's pot into play. All of it.

The sounds changed: some observers had gasped, some nodded, some laughed, and the sound trailed into the casino's sound systems and came back in a small wave, smoothed, bringing music of a deeper timbre and complexity from the hidden nerligig.

The Scout, afforded extra time to scan her hand, did so without complacency before making a small humming noise and matching the value of the pot. The rumble of some ship off port filtering through momentarily held them silent.

"Pilot, yes."

Quin nodded and picked up his cards, their feel in his hands all sharp-edged silk, peering at them to the exclusion of all else, pulling the numbers while one side of his brain calculated and the other side ruminated. A deeper portion of his mind sat behind it all, calmly measuring what he must do, encompassing at once three deep lines in the cards and the idea that really, there ought to be a place not quite beneath the space port's flight paths to play. . .

The Scout's first card hit the table with his as some other ship or plane lifted.

The nerligig added bass notes to the flow, and then his chances were measured. He'd felt the usual line come forward, and then the line Luken would play, and his grandmother's line. . .but there, his grandmother's was too knife edge, now, now that he'd seen the need to win. The usual line was too bland, and Luken's, well. . .there, Luken's line might add up to a stern chase. It would be interesting. Indeed, it *would* be interesting.

He let his gaze rise, let it wander the watchers, where some people had shifted, McFarland and Natesa perhaps a step closer. Villy, so intent that his flawless fair skin shone near as much as his hair, stood now in the first rank, with his Terran shadow an arms length row behind, towering.

The Boss was absent yet.

#

The line was clear enough to both of them by now: her chance was to shatter him with one of the three cards still to play, his was to lay down the whole of it by pulling two of hers. She considered. He did, and his hands moved without thinking, adding one more chip to the pile. Really, it didn't matter much if she folded now or showed her hand; his need was to have the pot without doubt.

His father was away from the play and away from monitors: as neutral as might be. Quin still had seen nothing more of the Boss. The Boss, cold enough to enter the turf of his enemies and show them down in their own office, drawing or not. But elsewhere for this test.

Natesa's glance had met his but once. She a Juntavas judge, a munitions expert, and. . .reputed merciless.

If there'd been a message in those eyes it had been "play on". . .and indeed, so he would.

"In for the Jump, pilot," the Scout said, matching his bet one more time.

Then she said, "The hotpad's yours, sir."

And, yes, it was.

He placed the blue *qe'andra* down, without flinching. If she answered in red or green this time, the hand was hers. If blue, there was a game still.

She showed the blue seven.

There was a sigh from the watchers—clearly some favored the Scout, or had at least committed money in that direction.

For his part, Quin kept his gaze at the table, and then he, followed with the lowly pivot, in blue. The point of it, really.

There was a murmur then, but she handily reached into her set and played the green pivot. It was, of course, one move too late. . .

He sighed. He'd had some concern, of course, but the pivot she'd played, been forced to play, one move late—

"The full Clan Royale, Scout, on my side."

Yes, she had a card, and the cards he laid down brought that last card to him, capping the delm as he knew it would, making the clan whole. He formally faced out his card to show her, to show the room, before slipping it into the spot.

She bowed where she sat, and then rose, and bowed again, full of intricacies he'd not seen for a relumma or more. No, this was Surebleak. He'd not seen such a bow for *months.*

Her bow offered equality with a touch of seeing an error, on her part, corrected. . .and she said then, "Your jacket fits you well, pilot. May you continue to command your boards so well!"

And she was gone, the noise starting as he sat, the satisfaction of the win tempered– there'd been a warning in that last from the Scout, and he must take it: he'd been on the edge of good taste with his boast, and she'd come within a card of proving him wrong. One card. On the other hand, he'd earned the win, proved the point. . .and now. . .

Natesa the Assassin stood by, with a simple bow covering the territory of, "I see you" and not much more. And there was Cheever McFarland, who held out a Terran style handshake to him, saying jovially, "Remind me not to play piket with you, if ever it comes to sit at a serious table. . ."

There too, was Villy, an odd grin on his face. Quin smiled, bare-ly hearing Villy's offer above the clamor: "You need something to eat, Pilot! You haven't had anything all day! Will you join me?"

How Villy might have kept track of that he didn't know, but true, Quin *was* hungry, and he felt a little shaky. His winnings were far beyond his quartershare and. . .he needed something to eat, and he owed Villy that tip!

Villy was moving slowly against the flow of the crowd, and there he was, suddenly, repeating himself as he came within arm's length.

"You haven't had any food all day! Will you join me?"

"He will not, Villy, at least not now. This pilot has kept me waiting."

Quin turned, saw Villy's face go white and kept turning, to find Boss Conrad himself at his shoulder.

"I trust you've not accepted another game? I'm afraid I've issued word that you're not to play cards here, other than private games, taken in parlor, until I say otherwise. It is unfortunate that you've become so angry!"

The statement was delivered quietly, with no bow to cushion or explain it.

Quin stepped back, appalled. He *had* entertained the idea of a challenge. . .

"So you'll not face me?"

"Beat anyone here at will, can you? It may be the case today, but you can't declare it! Do you know what that looks like, pilot? It looks that. . ."

Quin heard himself–

"It sounds that you're not up to the challenge, sir. Will you not play me, now if you like. . ."

Now his father took a step back, and Quin felt the roiling in his stomach going toxic. Cheever McFarland moved half between him and his father, and Villy's voice was close.

"No don't, that's the Boss! Don't make him. . ." Villy touched Quin's arm, surprising both of them.

"Villy," The Boss said, at the same time Quin managed–"Please. . ."

"I will play you if you will. Waiting for me? I've been waiting all day!"

Natesa's voice came low, and in Liaden.

"Perhaps this discussion should take place elsewhere."

McFarland's bulk gave way, and The Boss went on. There were people about, several still wishing to play the victor, others merely to talk, or to. . .

"I cannot play you here and you cannot play here in public and keep the Emerald's name clear!"

"Is that it? Nothing like cards is it? Well then let us simply have a contest. Twelve paces, one Terran Ace each, the shot takes the pip or is a loser. You've done that game at Tey Dor's!"

"It's the Boss!" Villy was now clinging to Quin's arm– "He can shoot better than. . ."

"He cannot beat me tonight, I warrant!"

Quin saw his father stand straight, suddenly. His face went formal, and there followed am intricate bow, a bow of–of a request for calm. Of a request to agree to dignity. Of acknowledgment of. . .something.

"I hadn't known that story was still current," his father said mildly. "However true it maybe, that was in other times, on another world. Here there are rules to enforce, and we do not allow gun play in the Emerald. We *cannot* allow it! We'd fetch proctors in an instant and *both* end up in the Whosegow."

Quin paused, realizing that, of course, the Rules were posted. No gun play. And that his father was now being some-what–amused.

Amused? What could. . .Quin stood taller, and half a step forward to press the issue, Villy like glue at his side.

The Boss went on, with gentle voice, close, for his ears, with a bow and hand motion indicating *stand down.*

"And yes, I did shoot that duel in Tey Dors. I won it, too. And, I admit, you can probably beat me at any game you name tonight–I've been up eighteen hours or more and you're full on the luck, as I can see." The Boss raised his hands palm up in a Terran gesture, a request for reason. "If the luck is on you, likely no one here can beat you! But you have stayed, and we will meet and have a meal. If you please."

Quin sighed, looked to Villy, who was watching him with some amaze—

"I told you I had a meeting. . .my party has arrived."

From nearby, there was a rumbling that was not a ship on launch but a grumble of a voice, deep and getting louder.

"I see it now, you're *all* in this. A trick, it was trick!"

Villy heard the man behind him, felt the crowd jostle and sway as they were pushed first toward the playing table and then against a large body, in angry motion. He heard complaints and then turned to see The Coat pointing at him and pushing in his direction.

"He's a sharp, a thief, he stole my money, him and his boyfriend connived it from me. They conned me. Give me my money!"

The Coat moved with more speed than Villy would have credited him with, sweeping cards from table and throwing chairs to both sides, cursing, moving forward.

Villy braced, felt a tug on his arm—

"Halt!" someone cried, and the tug powered him out of the man's path as the pilot sidestepped in and noise rose all about him. The crowd, depending on their type, ran toward or away from this sudden action and a distant bell went off; in the confusion someone in the crowd pushed and then someone else shoved and both the pilot and the coat were bowled over.

"Stop!" That was someone in security

The Coat was yelling and Villy saw him clambering over a half-dozen people, after him, "My money, give me my money!"

The pilot grabbed at The Coat's legs, knocking him down, half against Villy and then Villy saw the ominous black grip in The Coat's hands, and he reached for the gun while the man worked it out of the inner lining and–

The noise went on but the action on the floor froze.

The pilot was on his knees at The Coat's head, very shiny gun held steadily at the man's face.

"Drop the gun," he said in perfectly clear Terran, "or I'll kill you."

Villy heard and believed, his breath ragged.

The Coat looked into his face and Villy begged him "Just let the gun go or he'll do it!"

The noise was falling off now and Villy saw hands reaching in, a foot pinning The Coat's gun arm, and then arms and hand stripping the gun away, and then. . .

The pilot had to lean on him to get untangled, and rose, his gun disappearing as if it had never been drawn. The Coat was held now, Cheever McFarland's grip supplemented by others of the casino staff, and both Natesa and the Boss had their guns out, only to put them away.

The pilot–

Villy was awkwardly pulled up by strong warm hands, the pilot pushing a chair out of the way and helping him stand straight. Villy grasped the arm for support, getting his breath back, looking into the pilot's face to be sure he was unhurt.

"Stand down, man, stop struggling!" That was McFarland, who continued with, "Call the watch. I'll hold 'em, someone frisk him."

Villy felt a touch on his shoulder, ignored for now, as the pilot got his breath back and managed a wan smile. The touch on his shoulder grew firmer, and Villy glanced around, startled to realize he'd been ignoring Boss Conrad, who was smiling, and giving him an odd bow.

"Villy, please unhand my son. What you do on your time is yours, but for the moment, I owe him dinner and consideration, and something to do besides being a roving gambler."

Villy realized he still had a grip on the pilot's arm, but heard himself saying around his still somewhat ragged breath, "*Your son?*"

The Boss looked sidewise at the pilot –

"You two haven't been introduced? Villy. . ." He paused, then bowed between the pair of them in some formal way, "Villy Butler, I present to you one's son and heir, Quin yos'Phelium, Assistant Boss."

"Pleased to meet you," Villy managed, finally relinquishing his hold on the pilot's arm, reaching out automatically for the handshake, the while feeling stupid, oh, *stupid*. It was there in the face–in the attitude!

"Best pleased to be introduced!"

Quin's hand was firm but gentle, the shake honest and confident. Villy let go reluctantly, accepting and returning the nod and "Doyodo."

Quin's quiet–"I'll be looking you up soon!" surprised Villy, but then the Boss bowed to Quin, bowed to Villy–

"If you'll excuse us, Villy, we've a dinner waiting."

Villy nodded, watched them move toward the back rooms, and sighing, wondered when *soon* began.

* * *

The dinner did not, as Quin had more than half-expected, include Natesa, who'd last been seen discussing the scrum at the table with

Mr. McFarland. McFarland, for his part, had offered Quin, "That Villy's got a lot going for him. Went for the gun, right away. Saved us shooting the nitwit–saved you blowing his brains out!"

The Boss had agreed, bowed, and had interposed himself between Quin and the hubbub.

"This way, Quin my son, if you please," said his father and guided him down a hall and into a room Quin hadn't seen before, a plain and stain-free room, floor shining and walls proclaiming *new*.

There was a small desk, pushed somewhat aside to accommodate a dining table and chairs, opposite each other across the table, and ordinary settings from the Emerald's kitchen gracing a flawless green table cloth.

In the quiet, then, they stood at a proper Liaden distance from each other, his father's face changing expressions, far too mobile for Quin to decide what to do, and though it seemed as if his father didn't know what to say, either. His father was known for his address!

After too long a pause, his father bowed an unadorned bow of welcome between equals, and with a self-deprecating chuckle said, "The day was to have been simple and orderly, my son, and I discover that it has not been. Please, be seated. Dinner will be with us shortly."

Quin bowed acceptance, albeit warily, and seated himself, his father sitting quickly, and pouring a glass of wine for each of them.

They toasted the Tree-and-Dragon, and his father sipped with a ceremonial solemnity. Quin didn't recognize the bottle but knew it was excellent fare, and he nodded and heard himself sigh at it.

His father smiled, took another sip.

"Indeed. Indeed. Anthora gave me several of this bin, said to be a gift from Trealla Fantrol. How this might be so, I do not inquire, though I do not doubt."

Again a pause, and then. . .

"It strikes me, my son, that I have been. . .too busy. It strikes me, as well, that you have been busy at being busy. We must solve some of that, and soon. I hope you will hear me out."

He looked at the glass, put it down, and Quin put his down as well.

"Natesa has brought to me the consideration that you've been shunted about. We dragged you from your schooling, isolated you at Runig's Rock, then isolated you again at Jelaza Kazone. I thought it best to bring you to town so that we could begin preparing you for your role here as my heir–I told you that I would do so, in fact, but I did not ask if you wished it."

Quin bowed acknowledgment, carefully without irony.

His father sighed.

"Yes. I became Boss without asking Surebleak, and you are as caught in this as you were in Plan B."

Quin saw concentration flow across his father's face, and perhaps concern. The distant look became focused–focused *on him.*

"In the way of such things, my son, we are caught in the web of the world. You–*you* already have the skills to escape it one day, if that is your wish. In the meanwhile, we are here, and we are subject to the delm, because that is what we will."

Quin nodded–"Indeed, caught by the world, caught by history."

His father focused again, took a sip of his wine, then talk was suspended as dinner was wheeled in and set out.

"And here," his father said when they were alone again, "is where we vary, my son. The delm, in their wisdom, has put your grandmother to work on a very important project, a project important to us as a clan, to Surebleak, and to each of us, personally."

Quin allowed inquiry to show in tipping of the head.

"Kareen yos'Phelium Clan Korval," his father continued, "has been tasked to study–and if necessary, to advocate–the future shape and duties of Clan Korval, and those dependent on and from it."

Quin sat back into his chair, felt questions rising.

"But the Code. The Code tells us these things!"

His father showed a wan smile, and shook his head, Terran-style, in the mild-denial sense, and answered.

"The Code explicates proper behavior *for Liadens*. As a Liaden, with the consent of the delm, I was permitted to spend my life as a roving gambler. As long as I was an honest gambler, I was provided with a ship and a pilot, and could wander where I willed. My quartershare, was deposited in my accounts on schedule–as they still are. And on-world and off I was constrained by the Code used by Liadens."

Quin felt an emptiness, a gone feeling, not fear, but unease writ large.

"And now that we have been cast away, we are no longer Liadens?" he ventured. "But surely The Code. . .does it not hold?"

"Shall I expect it and enforce it? Shall you?"

The question lay between them as his father began removing the covers from his meal.

"If the Code is in force, you would need impose Balance on the Terran who mishandled Villy–he called you in collusion, the pair of you. Instead, according to Surebleak's Code, he goes to the

Whosegow, and you and he are done. Balance is thus achieved, though by Liaden lights it is no Balance at all."

His father looked up as he moved the plates around, offered across some bread. "Per the Delm's Word, I have left behind all of my Balances on Liad. As you should, though I doubt you have any of moment. And I say to you that Kareen yos'Phelium studies the question of what is proper behavior for Surebleak. If any should discover such things, it will be her."

Quin nodded a bow of acknowledgment: Grandmother was a legend in such matters!

"And so far," his father went on, "the fruit of her search brought back to the delm and to the clan, is that imposing the Code as we know it on Surebleak is indefensible."

"But here, before the meal cools, let me tell you that the delms intend the clan to continue until or unless they discover it should not. If it should do as Surebleak does, as many Terrans do, and become a family instead of a clan—they will see to that."

Quin felt somewhat better, began removing his own covers, dared a sip of wine, which was *still* excellent. And he—they—were not going to be simply clanless. . .and that also was excellent.

"And today, my son," his father said, "among all the other activity required for having the Port re-certified and also—by the way, upgraded three levels—today we had arrivals. New in orbit today, brought by Surebleak's fleet from deep storage, were three ships. One, named *LucyBug*, belongs to Cheever McFarland. Rarely has a man been so pleased!"

He looked up, saw the smile on his father's face, felt his own grow. His father dipped a hand in his jacket pocket, and held keys toward Quin. Ship keys.

"The other two arrivals are recently refurbished ships of the clan, *Galandasti* and *Mestro Tour.* Padi being away, you may look them over and choose which of these Jump ships you wish to fly as your own, when your duties and studies permit."

Quin nearly dropped the pair of them. So light and yet so weighty, he held them above his dinner in awe, looked into his father's face, found no words.

His father smiled. "How you will choose between them I do not know—they are of the same yard and year, and I'd swear the same polish."

"I do *hope*, as your father and as the Boss, that you will not choose to go a-roving quite yet. I do hope that Code or not, you will continue to acknowledge our connection."

"Of course, Father, how could I not?" he paused, found his voice gone and then returned— "I am proud, Father, to be of the clan. I see difficulties, but the clan—Grandmother, Grandfather, the delms—all, yes, all I cherish!"

Without thinking or looking, he closed his hand around one set of ship keys and handed the other back, and saw it accepted with a nod.

"The clan does well by us Father, and you do. I can only hope I can do as well by the clan, and by you. I am pleased to be your son. Of course I shall wait on my roving."

Code of Honor

"You wanted to see me, ma'am?"

Tech Sergeant Tommy Lee saluted, and waited for the captain to acknowledge him.

She looked up from her screen, eyes shadowed, and Tommy felt a pang. Cardimin had been hard on her; had been hard on all of them. He'd gotten a scratch out of it; Captain Blake had gotten. . .more than a scratch. She ought not even be out of sick bay–that was Tommy's opinion, and let the record show that he was *not* a medic.

"Sergeant." She nodded in return to his salute, and used her chin to point at the chair by her desk. "Sit down, please."

"Ma'am."

He sat, frowning up at her face. Drawn and looking older than she was. *Dammit, she ought to be resting!*

"Correspondence just come in regarding you," she said, looking down at her screen. "You know a Jow Lit pen'Chapen?"

For a moment, he thought to deny it; after all, who could say they knew the delm of clan Severt? Certainly not the least-valued of his grandchildren. But, no; it wouldn't do. She would have his record on her screen. Fifteen Standards he had served in her command, and *Tommy Lee* before he'd risen from the signing table; she'd need a reminder of his birth name.

So.

"Jow Lit pen'Chapen is Delm Severt," he said calmly. "My grandfather."

Captain Blake nodded.

"He sent a pinbeam to Commander Wyatt, stating that you're needed by your clan."

Ice ran his veins. The words hadn't quite made. . .

"I beg your pardon?"

She looked up then; looked right at him, and smiled, tiredly.

"Your grandda invoked the escape clause, Tommy. You're free to go home. Wyatt's already signed off on it."

But I don't want to go home! he thought, which might have been undutiful, had things been otherwise, between him and his clan. He did not say this to Susan Blake; it would do nothing but distress her.

She shifted, slightly, fretfully, behind her desk.

"Says here there's a transport voucher in your mailbox. You're to leave immediately, and travel with all haste. Apparently, there's specific instructions in your box along with that voucher." She sighed, and shook her head at the screen.

"Couple administrative things. . ." she murmured. "First is, you wanna close your account in the Merc Bank?"

Close his account? And what? Carry his entire savings in his pockets?

He shook his head.

"If it's possible to leave the account as it is, I would prefer to do that," he said. She nodded and touched a key.

"OK. What do you want us to do about mail? You can keep your box open. Be a fee– four-bit per Standard."

Hardly a fee at all, and certainly cheaper than renting a civilian box and paying for transfers and forwarding.

"I'll leave it open for now; the fee's acceptable. When I know what. . .my clan. . .requires of me, I'll be able to make a decision. . ."

Gods, it had been half a lifetime since he had thought like this. . .*what my clan requires of me*? He was accustomed to command; the merc culture suited him well. But merc culture–merc *disci-*

pline—was a shallow and meaningless thing when measured against the absolute power that a delm held over the members of his clan. A delm could order a kinsman shot for no reason other than he been found an irritant. No one would remonstrate with him, or demand that he explain himself, or call him to stand trial for violations against the reg book. . .

"Tommy? You OK?"

He took a deep breath and looked up to meet her eyes.

"Truthfully, I'm. . .shaken. Does he—Delm Severt—say what the clan requires of me?"

Even as he asked, a new fear iced his heart.

His mother.

Had his mother died? But surely he would not be called home merely to mourn her. A leave of absence, perhaps, but this. . .

"He's a man of few words, your grandda. Just the bare phrase, to do the necessary."

He shook his head.

"I don't accept his invocation of the Liaden Personnel Release Clause," he said, dragging the proper name of the provision from gods knew what pocket in his well-pocketed memory. "I'll make inquiries. If necessary, I'll arrange for a leave of absence. This is. . ."

The captain was shaking her head, and she was frowning the particularly fierce frown that meant she was unhappy, not angry.

"You don't get a say," she said. "Tommy, I checked. You *bet* I checked! Some old guy sitting on Liad's gonna take away the best palaver and protocol sarge this unit's ever had?" Another headshake. "It's got a whole chapter to itself in the regs: Liadens belong to their clan; if-and-when their clan says, *come home*, the merc's gotta cut 'em loose. No delay. No return."

No return.

He was speechless.

There was a small pause before Captain Blake sighed, and spoke again, her voice sounding infinitely weary.

"So, there's some things for you to sign here, Tommy. . ."

#

He arrived at Chonselta Port in the early hours of the morning, which suited him, and his plans. He found a tea shop and ordered breakfast, talking with the bored clerk while he ate. He'd taken the precaution of brushing up on modes and forms during the long days of travel, which was prudent, but left his ears tuned to the Solcintran accent. The Chonselta burr was at first disconcerting, then oddly comforting. He'd spent the last half of his life so far getting around in the various dialects of Terran and in Merc pidgen, with sometimes intense forays into other languages, as required by his duties. Of course, he'd spoken Liaden occasionally during the past fifteen Standards, but he had by no means spoken it every day. Doubtless, his grandfather would find him inexcusably rough, but that would be no new thing, and he was no longer an unskilled and despised halfling, but a man grown and secure in his accomplishments.

He reached for his tea cup; paused to look at the ring on the smallest finger of his right hand. It was a utilitarian thing, as ornaments went, the stone set flush to the band so as not to foul in wires, or catch on combat gloves. A Liaden would scarcely call it a ring at all, but for the honor it denoted; and perhaps not even then. He had another ring in his kit–a broad banded, heavily gemmed affair that he wore when attending official parties and meetings with planetary officials, and others who were impressed by such things.

Perhaps he should have it on, when he presented himself at the house.

That reminded him of his agenda, and he put the question to the clerk, who smiled and nodded significantly toward the left wall of the shop.

"Faces Spa will put you in the current style," she said. "Just three shops up, at the corner."

"Will they be open, so early?"

"Be shifting over to the day crew right about now," she answered, so he finished his tea, paid his tab, and walked up the street to have himself put into the current style.

#

After the spa, his braid shorn and the remainder of his pale hair arranged in soft curls over his ears, it was the tailor, who was pleased to serve Tom Lei pen'Chapen Clan Severt, and in very quick order produced a jacket, shirt, and trousers befitting the returning son of a mid-level House known to have ambitious tendencies. His good duty boots were changed out for a thinner, shinier pair, with a heel that would make marching painful. The tailor also produced evening clothes—"In the event that the House dresses for Prime"—and a second set of day clothes. In addition, he quick-cleaned Mr. pen'Chapen's travel leathers, sweater, and boots while the gentleman was in the dressing room, and had them waiting neatly on the counter when he emerged.

"I thank you," Tom Lei said, remembering to incline slightly from the waist—not quite a bow, but a modest genuflection to one who has performed an unexpected small service. He produced his purse, meaning to settle his account immediately, and was stopped by the tailor himself.

"By no means, sir! Clan Severt of course keeps an account here, and settles very promptly at the end of every relumma! I have no hesitation in appending today's modest purchases to this relumma's accountings."

"I thank you," Tom Lei said again, while, mentally, he sighed. Of course, Severt kept accounts with the local tailors. It was how things were done, on Liad. He, long-accustomed to drawing his uniforms from stores, and purchasing joy-clothes and civvies from his own funds, had simply assumed—but there! *This* was his uniform, now.

"I am happy to serve," the tailor was assuring him. "If you should need to expand your wardrobe—reception wear, or intimate items—please do not hesitate to call upon me."

"I will remember," he promised, and reached for his kit, to stow cleaned leathers and boots.

"May I call a cab for you, sir?" the tailor asked.

He had intended to walk from the tailor to Severt's Clanhouse, a matter of some several dozen blocks. Walking would have served two purposes: it would have consumed time, should that have been necessary, until an hour when the House could be expected to be awake; and it would have given him one last opportunity to prepare himself for the upcoming meeting with his grandfather.

Walking long blocks in these absurd new boots, however, was only likely to give him blisters and bad temper. And, too, the process of becoming presentable had taken rather longer than he had expected. The House would certainly be awake by this hour, and if they were still at breakfast, then he could certainly await his grandfather's pleasure in one of the small parlors.

"A cab would be most welcome," he told the tailor. "I thank you again, for your care."

#

Severt's Clanhouse was situated on Omarine Street; not in Chonselta's first neighborhood, but well enough. It was pleasantly tree-lined, and the houses sat back from the public walk, protected from the prying eyes of passersby by small gardens.

Tom Lei pen'Chapen paused with his hand on the gate, looking over the garden, and, if truth be told, the flagged walk that meandered from the gate through the flowers, to the stairway that ended at the front door.

In theory, his palm print was known to the security systems. Which, in theory, would open both gate and door to him.

Standing there, he knew a moment of hope, that the security system had forgotten him after all this time; that the gate would remain closed to him; so that he might have a reason to turn away, and resume his life. . .

But no.

His life as it had been was gone. His clan had need of him; his delm had called him home. Once more, he was merely a game piece, one among many interchangeable game pieces in his grandfather's endless quest for advantage.

He put his hand on the gate.

It swung open on well-oiled hinges.

He sighed, then, and settled his kit more firmly over his shoulder, before stepping into the garden, and following the path to the stairs.

#

The front door was opened, not by one of the House's children, but by a butler, unknown to him. He gave his name, and the information that the delm had called him home.

"I was told to expect you, sir," the butler said imperturbably. "The House is at breakfast. Will you join them at table, or will you await the delm's pleasure?"

He was a mercenary sergeant with sixteen world-falls to his account. On one memorable occasion, he and eight others of his squad had not only denied a prime target to a full platoon of the enemy, but routed them.

He was not by any means a coward.

But the thought of meeting his entire extended family at the breakfast table brought a cold sweat to his brow, and a decided uneasiness to his belly.

"Thank you," he said to nameless butler. "I breakfasted at the port. I will await the delm's pleasure."

"This way, then, sir."

He was led, not to the public receiving parlor, only a few steps from the door, but down into the house, until at last the butler opened the door to the delm's very office, and bade him be comfortable.

"Shall I have that taken to your rooms, sir?" the butler asked, by which he meant the kit bag Tom Lei yet carried. He surrendered it with a pang, refused the offered glass of wine, and, after the door had closed, wandered restlessly over to the shelves.

He was perusing the titles there when the door opened again, much sooner than he had anticipated, and a sharp voice exclaimed behind him.

"Well, you took your time getting here!"

Between one breath and another, his nerves steadied.

"I traveled with all haste, as instructed," he said, and turned to face his grandfather.

"It's been an entire relumma since I sent for you, sir!"

The old man hasn't changed a hair.

That was his first thought. His second was that his grandfather *had* altered: he was older, thinner, the hair that had still shown streaks of black when last they'd met was silver, now.

"It is the nature of space travel, sir," he said, speaking in the mode of younger to elder— *damned* if he was going to hold a conversation in clan-member-to-delm. And if he was going to be chewed out. . .

But his grandfather had apparently thought better of whatever else he had been about to say. Instead, he inclined his head, and moved to the desk.

"Pour for us," he said shortly.

With prompt obedience, Tom Lei moved over to the wine table, and paused, uncertain of his memory.

"Do you drink the red?" he asked, more or less at hazard.

"At this hour? Canary."

He located the bottle, poured two glasses, carried them to the desk and placed one by his grandfather's hand.

The old man picked up the glass, and glared up at him, dark eyes narrowed. They were not much alike, Tom Lei and his grandfather, which was the crux of the matter. Tom Lei was Festival-get, and the mark of his fair-haired, blue-eyed, pale-skinned sire was far too plain upon him. He had looked a veritable ghost among his numerous black-haired, ebon-eyed, golden-skinned kin, taller than the tallest of them by time he attained his twelfth name day.

Worse than all of that, he had the misfortune to be the child of grandfather's least-favored daughter, who he was pleased to style an imbecile, though how a woman who brought the clan the considerable benefit of her salary as a freight expediter could be thought an imbecile...

"Do not *loom*," his grandfather snapped. "Sit down."

He did so without comment, and sat holding the glass in his right hand.

"You look well enough," his grandfather said. "I had been concerned that you would require more polish. A word or two in the ear of your aunt Manza should see you set up in the wardrobe. Jewels..."

He frowned, his gaze falling on Tom Lei's all but naked hands, and he felt a pang, that he had not remembered to get the state ring out of his kit and put it on.

"What is that you have on your hand?"

The tone was more disgusted than curious, and a hot reply leapt to his tongue.

Then, he glanced at his right hand, and the small token he wore there, remembering faces he would never see again, comrades, lovers, and friends, and for their sake, he chose to answer moderately and do no dishonor to the ring.

"It signifies that I made sixteen world-falls as a mercenary, and saw action on each."

His grandfather frowned.

"Is that an honor?"

"It is...an accomplishment," Tom Lei said, and added, "among mercenary soldiers."

His grandfather sat back in his chair, hands steepled before him. His eyes were on Tom Lei as if he studied the merits of an art work set before him.

"Excellent. You will wear that ring." The frown returned. "Where is your clan necklace?"

"I had never had one," Tom Lei said, and felt the slow burn of old anger. "When I came fourteen, you told my mother to find me a suitable employment that was out of your sight and cost you nothing."

"Whereupon you joined the mercenaries," said his grandfather.

"*Whereupon*," he corrected, though he might more wisely have allowed his grandfather's history to stand, "we went first to the Healers, who tested me, and found that I might safely be trained as a servant in the Halls. That training would have required money, however.

"After the Healers, we went to the Scouts. I was tested and offered a scholarship to be trained in a specialty. The scholarship, however, was dependent upon a small donation from my House.

"With both of these options rejected by the delm–" *and*, he added to himself, *my mother with a new bruise on her face*—"then, yes, we went to the mercenaries, and I was enlisted as a 'prentice soldier. The results of the Scouts' testing came with me, and I was trained in languages and protocol." He did not say that the mercenaries had paid his mother a signing fee, of which she had given him half. He didn't know what she might have done with that money, and even after so long he feared to betray her to her father.

"The mercenaries do not appear to have taught you to curb your insolence," his grandfather observed, and continued with scarcely a pause. "Never mind. You will have a clan necklace; you will have everything that a son of Severt ought to have, and honor, too. You will be required to attend me. You will do as you are told, and you will say that which I give you to say. In this way you will bring benefit to your House, and increase our standing among the clans. Do you understand me?"

Well, no; he didn't. But, when had he ever understood aught about his grandfather save that the old man hated the sight of him, and considered him a drain upon the resources of the House?

"Yes, sir," he said, mildly.

His grandfather failed to look pleased. He stood, abruptly. Tom Lei came to his feet as well.

"Go and find Manza. Tell her that you'll want good clothes; that I intend to take you about and show you to everyone. Can you do that?"

"I believe it may not be beyond me."

Dammit, Tommy, hold your tongue!

He met his grandfather's black eyes, and waited for the explosion.

It didn't come.

"Leave me," his grandfather said.

Tom Lei bowed and left the room.

#

His aunt Manza was in her own office at the back of the house; a small room the one charm of which was the tall narrow window that gave out onto the back garden. She heard his grandfather's instructions with no expression on her face, reached into the middle drawer of the desk and withdrew a gold chain from which a golden icon in the shape of Severt's shield twinkled. He received it from her hand and slipped it on over his head without looking at the shield.

"The clothes you are wearing were got in Chonselta," she said then.

He nodded.

"This morning, at bin'Dekel's shop, on East Port Street," he said. "I thought it best, were I not to show up in my traveling gear."

His aunt smiled, faintly.

"You never were a fool," she commented. "So, since Master bin'Dekel has your measurements, as of this very morning, and since his work is perfectly unexceptional, I will call him immediately and order in those things Severt desires you to have. They will be sent up to your rooms when they are delivered." She turned to her screen, tapped a key.

"There is a small card party this evening to which I daresay you will accompany your grandfather, if you are to be shown to *everyone*." She looked at him appraisingly. "What you are wearing now will do, though it should be freshened. . ."

"I bought a second suit, much like this," he said, and she inclined her head in acknowledgment.

"Tomorrow night is pen'Valer's reception, for which you will need something more, but we will have it by then." She moved her shoulders. "You're in the back hall, second floor; the middle suite." Another glance, this one slightly softer. "It has much the same view as this room, and is quite the nicest suite on the hall."

She turned back to her screen; he was dismissed to quarters.

He stood his ground.

"Aunt."

She looked up, frowning.

"Where will I find my mother?"

The frown grew deeper and for an instant, he thought she would refuse to tell him.

Then she sighed, and shook her head.

"Your mother died six Standards ago," she said.

His mouth dried, and he had to ask it—*had* to ask it, though it brought dishonor on the House even to *think* the question.

"By Grandfather's hand?"

Aunt Manza came half out of her chair, her face richly flushed.
. .

. . .and sank down again, with something that might have equally been a laugh or a sob.

"We had all feared that, at one time or another," she said, as if to herself. "Why should Elza's son not have feared for her, too?" She met his eyes.

"Be at peace, child. She was struck by a lorry as she crossed the street in the port, on her way to work, late she was, that morning, and likely failed to look. The lorry driver said she darted out from between delivery vans in front of the market; he barely saw her, and had no time to stop."

He saw it, in his mind's eye. Saw her crouching between the vans; saw her gauge her chances. . .

"It was deliberate." It was a certainty, not a question. His grandfather might be a cipher to him, but he had known his mother well.

Aunt Manza's mouth twisted with old pain.

"Between us–I think it was, yes. We don't speak of it, here in the House. Most especially not to your grandfather."

A warning. He bowed.

"Thank you. I know you were my mother's friend."

She sniffed.

"Not enough her friend," she said quietly. She looked down at the screen and touched a series of keys.

"You will wish to inspect your room," she said. "If you have particular requirements, in terms of furniture or ornaments, please speak to me."

"Yes, Aunt," he said, and left her to her work.

#

Card party, breakfast fancy, afternoon gather, another card party. . .Had he not been trained to endure tedious social gatherings, he might have gone into a decline.

Happily, there was other employment for him. Aunt Manza stood as Nadelm Severt, which meant that his grandfather had piled all of the clan's administrative work upon her, thereby keeping himself free for intrigues and gambling with the clan's fortunes. He offered his assistance, and, after a long, considering look, his aunt had accepted it. This was how he had learned the state of the clan's finances.

"We ought to remove to the estate, and sell the town house," Aunt Manza told him, "but the delm will not hear of it."

No, of course not.

When he was not helping with the nadelm's endless work, he walked. Fifteen Standards as a soldier had left him unfit for the sedentary life of an office clerk, or a Liaden gentleman.

The exercise was at first the conscious part of his walking, but he found the ingrained habits of a soldier marking out the territory, and after day eight he knew short cuts and potential danger points, knew the corner across from the park where he'd likely find a proctor leaning within view of the public comm station, the corner where the halfling fashionistas flirted with any who might notice them. He avoided the park's mirror-pool, which reminded him only too much of Cardimin's pond-pocked city and the ugly house-to-house fighting there.

Had he not been on duty for the House, he might well have enjoyed the walks, over time. But no. During his walks, he turned over the conversations he was included into, as Delm Severt's grandson, as Delm Severt's secret weapon.

His grandfather had, indeed, an odd set of acquaintances, and peculiarly interesting for someone who had a particular training.

...as, for instance, his own training: not only to endure, but to listen to the unspoken conversations, and deduce the hidden strategies.

Before the end of the first card party, it was perfectly plain to Tom Lei that his grandfather had managed to ingratiate himself with some members of Houses that could only be called High. During the breakfast fancy, it also became plain that there was a secret project with which those same High Houselings required assistance; a secret desperate enough that they could not afford to be choosy regarding such minor matters as social standing or *melant'i*.

By the time he and his grandfather had returned home from the second card party, Tom Lei was quite frightened.

His grandfather was ambitious, yes. His grandfather had always been ambitious; and as a result, he had always played at stakes somewhat above his reach. That he was good at the game was evidenced by the fact that Severt had not plummeted into obscurity, but had actually made some small gains in the clan's social standing.

But this game—the game in which he, Tom Lei was somehow a high-stakes pawn—this game was dangerous even beyond his grandfather's understanding.

Korval was involved—and Korval was not—*was never*—to be considered anything less than dangerous, though they had been banished from Liad, and had only days remaining until their departure.

But there was more–something he couldn't *quite* hear, in the whispers between the words said aloud, but which made him shiver, nonetheless.

It was also plain that he, himself, was being vetted and passed up a ladder of individuals who were increasingly important in this business of whispers and secrets.

What he would find at the top of the ladder, he dared not guess.

#

After he had been four weeks in the house, he was called into the presence of his grandfather and his delm before the midday meal, and there received from him his instructions for the coming evening's entertainment.

"You will dress in your best. I will send rings; you will wear them on your left hand. On the right, only the honor-ring you have from the mercenaries. You will tonight be at my side; you will follow where I lead. Do you understand me?"

This is it, he thought; *this is the big one; all the smaller hurdles have been conquered.* Perhaps he ought to be proud of himself–of his skill–that he had been passed all the way to the top.

But what was he to do, he thought, alone in his rooms, after the rings had been sent up, and he had chosen three for his left hand. The course of honor, according to the Code, was to obey his delm. But if his delm was about to ruin the clan, by engaging in a game the stakes of which were higher than even the Highest Houses ought offer? Where was honor then?

On the few occasions when he had been required by his duty to operate at such rarefied heights, he had instructions; a goal; backup from a commander who had been bold, yes, but who did not gamble blindly, nor waste his counters.

No, he thought, staring down into the garden from his window. The goal must be to preserve the clan, if it came to that, tonight. He must prevent his grandfather from doing anything foolish. That must be his course. He was the only one of Severt able to stand against the delm; the rest had long ago been beaten down by his will.

Decision taken, he turned from the window and lay down on his bed, to nap and recruit his wits for the coming test.

#

"Lord ven'Astra, allow me to present my grandson, Tom Lei, newly returned to us after serving many years as a soldier in a Terran mercenary unit."

Lord ven'Astra was a spoilt-looking man in middle years. He wore High House hauteur like a cloak about his elegant shoulders, and looked at grandfather with a slightly bored air.

Tom Lei made his bow.

"Lord ven'Astra, I am honored to meet you," he said, once again grateful for the training that had taught him to lie with ease and conviction.

"Young pen'Chapen." The lord returned a nod, and looked momentarily thoughtful. "Newly returned from the mercenaries, are you?"

"Yes, my lord."

"Has your grandfather discussed our little conundrum with you?"

Well, this might be easy, thought Tom Lei. *Perhaps all I have to do is play the fool.*

"I don't believe that he has, sir," he said politely.

Grandfather stepped in.

"Indeed, we have not spoken on the topic. I wished him to hear it first from you, my lord, and to give you his untutored opinion. Everyone here knows that I think we must make an example, or lose *melant'i.*"

"Quite," said the lordship, and turned his full attention to Tom Lei.

"The situation is thus, young pen'Chapen. There remain in custody several mercenary soldiers—perhaps a half dozen—hired by Korval to invade our homeworld and assist in the action against Solcintra. There are those among the Council who believe that we should release these. . .persons to their units. And there are those among the Council who believe that we should make, perhaps, not an example, but a statement. And that statement would be that Liad is not a paltry world that may be invaded at will by Terrans; and that consequences attend such outrages."

Tom Lei felt cold, hearing the whisper behind the words.

Those others, which included this lord and his grandfather, wished to execute the mercenaries in the Council's custody.

"The information that reached my unit regarding the strike against Liad," Tom Lei said carefully, "was that the mercenary units which supported Korval's action were properly hired by, and under contract to, Clan Korval. Was this not the case?"

"The contracts were produced as evidence," Lord ven'Astra acknowledged. "Korval had hired them. That does not set aside the fact that they performed outrages against Liad and its citizens."

"Indeed," his grandfather said. "It must be made plain that we will not tolerate it."

"Do you agree, young pen'Chapen?"

But this was absurd! The man went against...

"Law and custom have long held that mercenaries properly under contract are in the same class as weapons used in acts of lawlessness: blameless tools. The hiring body is seen by law as the motivating force—the finger that pulls the trigger, if you will—and is therefore the responsible party in all legal actions."

"Tom Lei, you do not properly comprehend the case." His grandfather was sounding somewhat breathless. "These. . .creatures! dared to move against Liad."

"Yes," he said patiently, watching Lord ven'Astra's eyes; "because the contract required them to do so. It was not what we—the mercenaries—call a *blood war,* in which there is no contract, nor client, and the units act upon their own recognizance.

"In this case, the Terran mercenaries took contract with Korval. They did not invade wantonly, but in good order, in support of Korval's action, as required by the contract. If the Council of Clans must have more blood—" He made a small bow, as if embarrassed by his lapse, and spoke to Lord ven'Astra.

"Your pardon, sir; I fear that I may have been too long among the mercenaries. Allow me to say, instead, that if the Council of Clans feels that banishment is not Balance enough for the wrongs visited upon the homeworld, then the Council of Clans must re-open its case against the Dragon."

Lord ven'Astra pressed his lips together, his spoiled face grave.

"The *qe'andra* do not allow it," he said, and it was anger Tom Lei heard beneath the words. "There were those of us who wished to see Korval themselves executed, the Dragon's assets come to the Council, and those remaining set to work off the debt of repairing the damage. We argued for that, hotly. Alas, the Dragon had too many friends on Council. Execution was made into banishment, and confiscation of assets became divestiture.

"Now, the *qe'andra* rule that, as Korval has been given the actions it must perform in order to enter into Balance, said actions having a strong deadline attached, to introduce a secondary Balance at this juncture would itself be out of Balance."

"Even now, reduced as they are, Korval has the *qe'andra* in their pocket," his grandfather put in. "Why, dea'Gauss is the chair of their council! The Terran mercenaries have no *qe'andra*."

"Which does not make them guilty of war crimes, sir!"

Tom Lei felt ill. What did his grandfather hope to gain from this? ven'Astra's patronage? A blind man could see what *that* would be worth, once his lordship had a piece upon which he could place the blame, if opinion and law went against him. . .

"You seem decided in your opinion, young pen'Chaben," his lordship said, his voice decidedly cool. He looked aside.

"I suppose," he said to Severt, "that we must expect youth to be idealistic. It is a failing they soon grow out of."

"Precisely, my lord. I had been certain that Tom Lei was past such kittenish ways!"

"Obviously not." Lord ven'Astra looked back to Tom Lei, his eyes cold. "I would say that you are correct, sir."

Tom Lei bowed slightly.

"In what way, my lord?"

"You *have* been too long among the mercenaries. Severt, a good evening to you."

Lord ven'Astra strolled away into the depths of the gather, and Tom Lei was left alone with his grandfather's disbelieving stare.

#

"Tomorrow!" his grandfather shouted. "Tomorrow, you will go to Lord ven'Astra, and offer him your services!"

"My *services*?" Tom Lei looked at the old man in astonishment. "As an executioner, perhaps?"

"Do not be insolent, boy! This situation can be rescued–will be rescued. You need only do as you are told.

"You will go to his lordship and you will prostrate yourself. You will tell him, that upon talking the matter over with your elders, and thinking on it overnight, you understand that the insult carried to the homeworld by these Terrans must be Balanced. You will say that you are willing to testify, as a former mercenary familiar with law and custom in such matters, before the Council of Clans."

"His lordship will scarcely want that!"

"Silence! You will of course testify that law and custom support the execution of barbarians who force an invasion upon Liad."

Tom Lei stared.

"That," he said, his voice perfectly flat, "I will never do."

His grandfather spun around.

"You will do it, because that is what your delm requires of you!"

"No, sir. I will not dice with lives for your ambition."

"Will you not?" The old man stalked across the rug, until they were toe-to-toe. He thrust his face up into Tom Lei's.

"You will do as your delm requires, or you will find you have no delm at all!"

"That," Tom Lei heard someone say in perfectly calm tones, "is acceptable."

"Oh, is it?"

Tom Lei waited, feeling utterly calm. Severt would never bend before such a challenge, he thought. He must conclude the threat.

But, after a moment, his grandfather drew a breath, stepped back and walked across the room.

"A glass of wine will do us both some good," he said, and poured with his own hands.

Tom Lei, caught between relief and dismay, crossed to the wine table and received his glass.

"So," said Severt, when they had each sipped and lowered their glass. "I see it. You were accustomed to command, a little. You were, perhaps, accustomed to being given reasons for the actions you were commanded to perform, so that you might improvise, when and if necessary. Of course, it is difficult for you to drop such habits, which have, as I must surmise, since you stand here hale before me, served you well for many years."

He paused.

Tom Lei inclined his head and murmured, "Yes, sir," which seemed, by far, the safest course. It would seem that he was not to be cast out and declared dead to clan and kin. Or, at least, not immediately.

He mistrusted his grandfather in this eldritch mood. On the other hand, he entertained liveliest curiosity regarding what, in fact, the old man was about. Surely, *surely*, the reality was nothing so horrifying as his suspicions. Let him *know*, and perhaps he might sleep easier.

"Know, then, that the work which is underway, and to which I have recruited your assistance, will result in a great improvement the clan's *melant'i*. Once the thing is done, we will rise into the circle of the High Mid-Clans. At least, we shall ascend to those ranks. It is not out of the question, that Severt may, as a result of this action, rise to High House."

Tom Lei blinked.

"And who shall fall?" he asked, for it had been fixed for. . .a very long time, that there were but fifty High Houses.

"Fall? Ask, rather, who will rise!"

Tom Lei knew that he was not a fool. However, it took him more than a heartbeat to realize that his grandfather expected–no! Knew for a certainty!–that at least one clan would seek to rise into Korval's place. For *that* was how it was said: *There are precisely fifty High Houses. And then there is Korval.*

"Korval occupied a. . .unique place because of their contract," he pointed out.

Severt shrugged. "A contract may be trumped by contacts. And how refreshing to have a true Liaden clan, rather than a hireling, in that most unique position, eh?"

Tom Lei raised his glass, so that his failure to agree might pass unnoticed.

"So," said his grandfather and his delm again, after he, too, had partaken of his glass. "I will tell you now that these Terran mercenaries whose fate is to become an example for all of Liad's inferiors–they are hidden, of course."

"Of course," Tom Lei murmured.

"And, here is the point upon which our own ascension turns." His grandfather leaned close, and lowered his voice so that Tom Lei needed bend at the waist in order to hear.

"We, Clan Severt, hold the prisoners, in trust for ven'Astra."

Shock jolted him. He had been a fool to hope that the truth were less terrible than his imaginings. He had been a fool to think that his grandfather would be content to gamble only with lives. No, like any gambler, he must ever increase his stakes.

And, now, he diced with Severt's very existence.

"Does Aunt Manza know this?" he demanded.

"Am I a fool to share such a thing abroad? She knows nothing."

Relief warred with horror. He took a breath, trying to recruit his thoughts.

"Peace, peace," his grandfather said, perhaps reading distress on his face. "Whether the scheme is executed, or the mercenaries are returned to their officer, as the *qe'andra* have ruled, our safety—and thus our reward—is secure.

"Only think! If the matter falls out as ven'Astra wishes, then we are rewarded for our help. If the *qe'andra* prevail, ven'Astra will be grateful to us for keeping our knowledge to ourselves." He smiled, and sipped wine.

"Indeed, I am almost wishful that the *qe'andra* might take the point, for there is a limit to the rewards for good service, and none at all, as I have been able to find, to the amount that will be paid in order to preserve one's honor."

Tom Lei saw it in a flash, then. His grandfather was not merely foolish; he was a bad delm, actively dangerous to his clan and those who rested in his care. Indeed, when had Severt ever cared for those who resided under his hand? Only see Aunt Manza, ceaselessly at labor with neither thanks nor input into the clan's business, her joy broken. Or his own mother, dead by her own choice, rather than endure any more abuse from this delm who was no delm at all! Or—yes!—himself, flung away as useless; his new life broken without a thought to his well-being, when he suddenly came to hold value as a game piece!

"Well?" said his grandfather, false delm. "Now you have the reasons, and the rewards laid down. What think you, now?"

He took a breath, meaning to say that his refusal stood, that he would welcome death rather than continue in such a clan, with such a delm.

. . .and he took another breath, thinking, indeed, of his mother, and his aunt, and all those caught in the supposed care of this man. He thought of the Code, and the section dealing with those things that are owed, by an individual, to one's clan; and those other things, which are owed, by a clan, to its members.

He looked down into his grandfather's face, and he made answer, gently, in the mode of obedience to the delm.

"I would see these prisoners, that Severt holds in care for Lord ven'Astra. And I would see Lord ven'Astra, so that I may, indeed, place myself at service in the matter of their proper disposition."

His grandfather smiled.

"Excellent! We will tomorrow pay a morning call to his lordship, after which we will together go to the farm—"

He dared to lift a hand. His grandfather paused, and gestured for him to speak.

"I wonder if it might not be profitable, for all of us to meet at the place the prisoners are being kept. Lord ven'Astra may have those things which he may wish to convey to those whose lives he holds, in order that they have a clear understanding of their situation. I am an expert in languages."

His grandfather smiled again.

"And thus we demonstrate immediately your willingness to assist! Yes! It is well-thought. I shall arrange it!"

"Thank you," Tom Lei said, and bowed, gods help him, honor to the delm. He straightened.

"If we are done, sir, I will leave you. The night is fine, and I have not yet had my walk."

"Ah, the energy of youth!" His grandfather <u>laughed</u>. "When this matter is done, and we have our rewards, we must see you married—yes! To a proper daughter of the High! *That* will fix us well, indeed!"

He moved toward his desk, fluttering his fingers.

"Go, go; have your walk. Only take care that you are sharp for our meeting tomorrow!"

"Never fear, sir. I shall be as sharp as an Yxtrang's grace blade."

#

Lord ven'Astra was to meet them at the place—at Severt's own estate. That suited Tom Lei, who drove the clan's lumbering landau, less than half-listening to his grandfather's instructions regarding his demeanor toward his lordship, and the tenor of his apology.

"Do not be afraid to be bold—a mercenary's plain speaking will stand you well with him. You saw how it is with him, last evening, I think. He does not care to be gainsaid, but he likes a forthright manner. Only do whatever he asks you—and he will ask something, as a test against your changed opinion!—show yourself able and willing and all may be recovered."

Yes, certainly, Tom Lei thought, and glanced at the map on the dashboard to see how far yet they had to go.

At last they arrived. His grandfather had him drive past the house, and his stomach tightened, for he knew then where they were going, and the riddle of how a group of seasoned mercenaries were held was answered.

Some generations in the past, the delm had traveled to some or another far outworld and there became introduced to the sport of hunting to the hounds. So enamored of this sport had she become that she imported her own pack, and keeper, and every relumma hosted a hunt throughout the neighboring fields.

The dogs—quite fierce dogs, who bonded to the pack, of which they considered their keeper, but no other human, a member—the dogs required kennels. And the kennel, given the temper of the dogs, was required to mete out stern discouragement of escape.

Once the dogs were kenneled, a switch was thrown, which electrified every floor, every wall, every surface, save those in the dog pens, proper. An escape from the den room into the main hall, would be rewarded by a jolt of energy sufficient to stop the heart of a being far larger than a hunting dog.

The dogs were sold off by the delm's successor, but the kennels had endured.

"Here," his grandfather said from the seat next to him. "Stop here."

#

He had scarcely stopped their vehicle, when Tom Lei spied the approach of another. Moments later, Lord ven'Astra emerged from the small car he had driven himself.

"Severt," said his lordship. "Good morning to you."

"A delightful morning, indeed, my lord," his grandfather responded.

The cool eyes came to rest on Tom Lei, who bowed as one who has discovered oneself in error.

"Your delm tells me that you have undergone a change of ideology, young pen'Chapen. Is it so?"

"My lord, it is," Tom Lei answered.

"It gratifies me to hear you say so. Let us by all means survey the prisoners, and you may do a small thing for me, if you will."

"Certainly, my lord," Tom Lei said calmly.

\#

There were six mercs in the large den room. The water was running in the drinking pool; and a light on inside the basic sanitation unit that had been installed for the use of the hounds' keeper on the not-infrequent nights when she slept with the pack.

The six prisoners–Terrans, all–looked well enough, though pale. They wore what appeared to be house robes, which were short in length and sleeve, leaving legs, and wrists, and bare feet on display.

"Well, if ain't Mister Bully-for-Me and Uncle Me-too," said a voice in Aus-dialect Terran.

Tom Lei glanced at his two companions. If either one understood the dialect, or the insults to themselves, they chose not to react, which seemed like neither of them.

Tom Lei felt his heart lift, slightly, and he turned again toward the former den, one hand against the plexglass window and the other at belt height, fingers dancing lightly in merc sign.

The man who had spoken–his robe so short as to be immodest, and his beard in need of a good trimming–lifted an eyebrow, and braced his feet wide.

"That one," Lord ven'Astra said, "with the hair of his face almost touching his chest. He is a leader of some sort; the others listen to him. I would have you translate my words to him, young pen'Chapen; *exactly* my words. Will you do that?"

"Yes, sir," he said, meeting the Aus' eyes calmly. He winked, and saw the man's other eyebrow rise.

"Excellent. First, tell him who I am."

"Yes, sir," he repeated, and spoke in the thickest, most incomprehensible Aus dialect he knew.

"Do you understand me?"

"Y'sound just like my old grandpaw."

"Excellent. The man with the brown hair, beside me, is a lordship. He's instrumental in keeping you here, and if he has his way you'll die, on camera, as a warning to others who'd invade Liad."

"We had a contract," the Aus said.

"He chooses to ignore that. He's going to give me words to say to you, now. Remember that they're his words, and reflect only his opinion."

The Aus nodded, and Tom Lei turned to his lordship.

"I have explained to him who you are, my lord."

"Excellent. Now, say this to him, and tell him to tell the others." He took a deep breath, and began to speak, rather too rapidly for a translator.

"Tell him that their officers no longer seek them; their names have been written out of the rolls of their companies and their families have been notified of their deaths," said Lord ven'Astra. "Tell them that their only remaining hope of honor is to confess before the Council of Clans that they are captured invaders of Liad, and pay the price named."

Tom Lei repeated it, as near as he was able, in that thick Aus accent. When he was done, the man before him asked a question.

"Is he nuts?"

"Might be," Tom Lei said. "What's important now is that his clan's powerful, and he wants all of you dead, publicly, to demonstrate his power and Liad's might."

The Aus glanced behind him, where the rest of his comrades stood silent.

"Two medics, two newbies, and a couple grunts," he said. "Some invasion force."

"Your lives are precious," Tom Lei said, which was something of a risk, but he would think of something to tell him, if ven'Astra asked to know what he said. "I won't let him harm you."

"You got point, brother," the Aus said. "I'll tell 'em now, unless there's something more. Any on your side speak Merc pidgin?"

"I think not."

"Have to risk it."

The Aus turned his back and approached the little knot of his comrades.

Tom Lei turned to Lord ven'Astra.

"If one may ask, my lord, how do you intend to execute them?"

ter'Astra was staring into the den, at the prisoners, a look of revulsion plain upon his face.

"I had expected that the Council of Clans would, eventually, be willing to see the deed done, but I learn only this morning that the Council will not even hear us. Other arrangements are being made, even as we speak. These will know full Balance within the next relumma, and all the galaxy will know what it is to trifle with Liad."

"Stand where you are, and place your hands on your heads," an authoritative female voice commanded. This was followed by a definite snap, as if of a safety being thumbed off.

ven'Astra half-turned; the voice told him to stop or accept the consequences, and a form stepped out of the hall behind them.

She was dressed in the neat business attire of a *qe'andra*. Her bow was crisp and unafraid. Her weapon was military grade, and held with confidence.

"I am Fantile dea'Starn," she said, calmly. "In this matter, I represent the planetary council of *qe'andra*. You will come with me."

"Where would you take us?" demanded Severt.

She considered him calmly.

"I would take you to our council chambers, where you will present evidence. There will of course be Healers present, to ensure that your evidence is presented in good faith."

"Thank you, madam," said ven'Astra. "You will only need these men here–" He nodded at Severt and Tom Lei. "These poor creatures are, as you see, imprisoned on the property of Clan Severt."

"Mine, is it!" shouted Severt. He swung out, his hand diving into his pocket.

Tom Lei lunged, snatched the arm up, brought the wrist sharply against his own forearm, and watched the gun fly from suddenly senseless fingers as he continued moving the arm, up behind the old man's back, heedless of his scream, and stood holding him.

"My thanks," said Fantile dea'Starn, and looked to her left. "Proctors, please, do your duty."

Lord ven'Astra lunged then, too late. One of the proctors swung something against his knee, and calmly caught his shoulder and snapped on binders as the afflicted knee buckled.

Tom Lei relinquished his grandfather to the second proctor, who likewise bound his wrists. He waited with the *qe'andra*, and the third and fourth proctors while the prisoners were escorted out.

"Thank you for your information," Fantile dea'Starn said, with a small bow. "The *qe'andra*, and also Korval, are in your debt."

She turned toward the den, where six pairs of eyes were watching the proceedings with very evident interest.

"Please," said Fantile dea'Starn, "tell them who I am and what has transpired. Tell them, too, that Liaison Officer Oshiamo is on his way to them even now from the port. He was delayed in traffic."

She used her chin to point at the comm on the third proctor's belt.

"If they wish it, we may call him; I have his code."

"Yes, ma'am," Tom Lei said, and turned to address the mercs.

#

Aunt Manza was Severt now; the *qe'andra* had quietly overseen the transfer, and duly recorded it. Grandfather was confined to his rooms.

"When we return to the estate," Severt said, "then he may find occupation that will risk no one."

"But you, Tom Lei—advise me, what shall I do?"

They were sitting together in the evening in her office, the same office overlooking the back garden, for, as she said, it was no use to move all of her work to grandfather's old office when she would only have to move it again, when the house was sold and the clan removed entirely to the country house.

"I ask," he said slowly, "that the delm kill me."

She blinked.

"That is hardly the Balance I should have suggested for such a service to your clan."

He shook his head.

"Aunt, consider: Lord ven'Astra is High House. There are others of his opinion who know me. Any one of them may decide that my betrayal of his lordship deserves the true death. It is not wise to have a target living among the clan, for sometimes even skilled assassins miss and the innocent are harmed." He gave her a wry half-smile.

"Notice that I do not dare speculate what terrors Grandfather would attempt to visit upon me!"

She chuckled, but protested anew.

"And, yet, for us, your kin, your clan—you have largely done good," she said, and again he shook his head.

"I presumed to judge the delm, and I found him wanting. I laid a trap and caught him." He leaned forward and touched her arm lightly.

"I am not safe for you, Aunt. How can either of us know that I will not do the like again?"

She laughed, and sat a moment, sipping her tea and thinking.

Finally, she sighed, and put the tea cup aside.

"You are determined that we mourn your loss, and I find that I must agree." She paused. "Very well, I will do it. But, first, you will tell me how long it will take you to be safely off-planet."

"I beg your pardon?"

"You, who have thought of so much, did you not think of this? If you are correct, and Lord ven'Astra's co-conspirators wish Balance, I will not give them a clanless man as a target. Once you are off-planet, then will Severt publish its sorrow abroad."

He inclined his head, chastised and pleased. Aunt Manza would be a good delm. She might even recover the clan's fortunes.

"I can be off-planet within the next day," he told her.

"Tell me when your plans are complete, and the time when your ship will lift. Now," she said, briskly. "You will take all that is yours, naturally, including the clothes the clan provided to you. There is no one here who they will fit, and you will need clothes, wherever you go, and whatever you may become. You will, in fact, take anything that is in your room which catches your fancy. In addition, you will take the rings that your grandfather gave to you—"

"But—" He began the protest, and swallowed it as she fixed him in her eye.

"You *will take* the rings your grandfather gave to you. Rings can be sold or bartered, and if your delm is to do as you command, my child, she cannot send you off with your pockets full of *cantra* pieces. In the meanwhile. . ."

She rose and bowed gratitude, as he scrambled to his feet.

"Severt thanks you for your service, Tom Lei pen'Chapen," she said, and straightened before he could return her courtesy.

She smiled then and opened her arms.

"Come now, child, and give your aunt your kiss."

This he did, willingly, and hugged her until she gasped a laugh and called him a great lout, and reached up to touch his cheek, tears in her eyes.

"Go and pack," she said softly. "I know you are eager to be away."

#

He dressed in his leathers and sweater, packing his new clothes, though they were far too fine for a merc. He touched his vest then, and heard the crackle of paper from the inside pocket, and smiled. The print out of the letter from the *qe'andra*, detailing his part in the rescue of the captive mercs, and another, from Liaison Officer Oshiamo, which had also been forwarded to Headquarters, to be appended to his file.

Yes, he was eager to be away. Away to Headquarters, where he intended to sue for re-enlistment with these letters, and the proof that he would never be called home by his delm again.

He wanted none of the ornaments in the room; he packed the rings, promising himself that he would sell them at the earliest opportunity. Then he straightened and looked about him, for anything else that was his.

There, on the bureau was. . .

He approached, and found three *cantra* pieces in a neat stack before a folder of holograms. A chill ran his spine; he picked the folder up, flipped it open, and. . .

. . .there was his mother, younger than ever he had known her, a progression of images, a few with Aunt Manza, a few more with him, and more, now older than he had known her, looking weary and thin. . .and another of them together. She was smiling, and he was, and she was holding an untidy bouquet of wildflowers that he had picked for her.

He flipped to the next page, but there were no more pictures, after.

Swallowing around the tears lodged in his throat, he slipped the little folder into an inside pocket of his vest and sealed it up. He picked up the *cantra* pieces as an afterthought, and dropped them into his public pocket.

#

Miri Robertson Tiazan Clan Korval, aka the Road Boss, on alternate business days, sat in her designated booth in the back of the Emerald Casino in Surebleak Port and tried not to be bored.

It was tough. Bidness was so slow, she'd even read all the outstanding reports and bulletins, and answered a couple of not-exactly-burning inquiries.

She wished that she dared take a nap; she *was* tired, and her back hurt, though not enough to make her swear that she was going to find whoever'd though it would be a good idea to get pregnant and dislocate their jaw.

She sighed. Maybe just a quick nap, with her head on the table. Couldn't hurt, could it, and Nelirikk, leaning against the wall by the booth like he could do it all day–which, he prolly could–he'd tell her if there was company–

A step sounded in the little hallway just beyond her booth.

Miri turned her head.

Nelirikk straightened away from the wall, and put his hand on his sidearm.

A shadow cleared the hall, resolving into a fair-haired man on the short side of tall for a Terran, and on the tall side of tall for a Liaden. He was a bit paler in the face than your usual Liaden, the fair hair pulled back into a tail. Dressed in merc leathers and good marching boots. Looked tired.

He took note of Nelirikk real quick, and stopped where he was.

"I am," he said, addressing both or either of them, "here to see Delm Korval."

"Well," said Miri, giving Nelirikk the hand-sign that meant *let the boy come closer*, "you found half of Delm Korval, though this is the Road Boss' office."

A Terran would get impatient with what would sound to him like plain and fancy nonsense; a Liaden would parse the information she'd just given him.

He inclined slightly from the waist.

"I beg your pardon. Is there a more appropriate time and venue to speak with Delm Korval?"

And that answered that.

Miri smiled.

"Happens things is slow this afternoon, so I'll do us both a favor and switch hats," she told him. "What's your name?"

"Tommy Lee," he said.

Well, so much for having him figured.

"You a merc?" she asked.

"*Former* merc," he answered and there was some bitterness there.

"What makes you former?"

He sighed, all of a sudden just looking weary of everything, but he gave her a clean enough answer.

"My delm called me home."

"That'll do it," she acknowledged. "Whatcha been doin' lately?"

That got a faint smile.

"*Most* lately, I have been suing for re-enlistment," he said.

"In my day, there wasn't any re-enlisting from the escape clause."

"Yes, but you see, I'm dead, and no longer subject to being called. . .anywhere." He smiled again, a little brighter. "It did go all the way to an All-Commanders Tribunal before it got denied."

"Well, that's something, yeah. So, what do you think I can do for you, Tommy Lee?"

He straightened into attention.

"I wish to offer my gun to Korval," he said formally.

Like a thousand others. Miri didn't sigh.

She opened the portable computer and tapped a key.

"What's your name?" she asked, her eyes on the screen.

"Tommy Lee."

She raised her head to glare at him.

"What's the name you enlisted under?" she asked with exaggerated patience. "Or maybe you got an ID number?"

He gave her the number; she entered it, and. . .blinked at the screen.

"Tommy Lee, sit down."

He did so, settling his pack neatly next to the chair.

Miri finished reading the file, then met his eyes over the edge of the screen.

"Been wondering for a while now what happened to the guy who pulled mercs out of a hat for us. We offered what help we could when they went missing, but by that point our help was worse than none, if you take my meaning. The mercs and the *qe'andra* took it and ran with it, but it was pretty much a dead end until some guy called up Ms. dea'Starn and told her he was going to be able to lead her to the prisoners."

She shook her head, glanced down at the screen, and back to him.

"Looks like we owe you, Tommy Lee."

"I came," he reminded her gently, "to offer Korval my gun. If you'll have it."

"We might. Have to talk it over with my partner, naturally. Tell you what. I got another couple hours on-duty here. When's the last time you ate something wasn't bar rations?"

He blinked.

"It's been a. . .while."

"Thought so." She looked at her aide. "Beautiful, take this man down to the kitchen and see him fed, then take him over to Audrey's for a nap. Bring him back here at quitting time."

"Yes, Captain. I will call House Security for your back-up here."

"Good idea."

She returned to Tommy Lee, sitting quiet and maybe a little wide-eyed in his chair.

"You'll come up to the house with me; have a little talk with us and with our head of house security, see if there's a way we can do each other some good. That OK by you?"

He swallowed, his eyes a little damp, maybe, but the grin this time was good and firm.

"Yes, Captain," he said. "That's OK by me."

ABOUT THE AUTHORS

Maine-based writers **Sharon Lee and Steve Miller** teamed up in the late 1980s to bring the world the story of Kinzel, an inept wizard with a love of cats, a thirst for justice, and a staff of true power. Since then, the husband-and-wife have written dozens of short stories and twenty plus novels, most set in their star-spanning, nationally-bestselling, Liaden Universe®.

Before settling down to the serene and stable life of a science fiction and fantasy writer, Steve was a traveling poet, a rock-band reviewer, reporter, and editor of a string of community newspapers.

Sharon, less adventurous, has been an advertising copywriter, copy editor on night-side news at a small city newspaper, reporter, photographer, and book reviewer.

Both credit their newspaper experiences with teaching them the finer points of collaboration.

Steve and Sharon are jointly the recipients of the **E. E. "Doc" Smith Memorial Award for Imaginative Fiction** (the *Skylark*), one of the oldest awards in science fiction. In addition, their work has won the much-coveted **Prism Award** (*Mouse and Dragon* and *Local Custom*), as well as the **Hal Clement Award for Best Young Adult Science Fiction** (*Balance of Trade*).

Sharon and Steve passionately believe that reading fiction ought to be fun, and that stories are entertainment. Steve and Sharon maintain a web presence at http://korval.com/

NOVELS BY SHARON LEE AND STEVE MILLER

The Liaden Universe®

Fledgling
Saltation
Mouse and Dragon
Ghost Ship
Dragon Ship
Necessity's Child
Trade Secret
Dragon in Exile
Alliance of Equals
The Gathering Edge
Neogenesis

Omnibus Editions

The Dragon Variation
The Agent Gambit
Korval's Game
The Crystal Variation

Story Collections

A Liaden Universe Constellation: Volume 1
A Liaden Universe Constellation: Volume 2
A Liaden Universe Constellation: Volume 3

The Fey Duology

Duainfey
Longeye

Gem ser'Edreth

The Tomorrow Log

by Sharon Lee

Barnburner
Gunshy
Carousel Tides
Carousel Sun
Carousel Seas

THANK YOU

Thank you for your support of our work.

Sharon Lee and Steve Miller

Made in the USA
Coppell, TX
13 February 2020

15758124R00060